Ravenwood

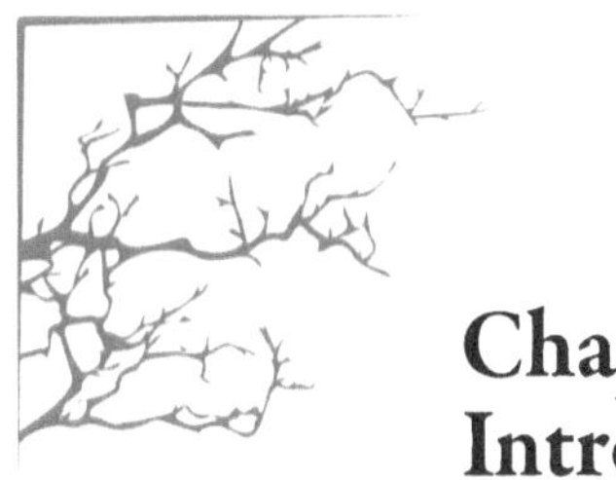

Chapter One
Introduction

Along Route 116, miles away from the nearest town where the state road curved and weaved its way through the backwoods of Massachusetts was the lane that would take you to Ravenwood. It would be easy to miss if you weren't looking for it or didn't know how to follow directions. The trees had grown taller since it was built making it no longer visible from the main road. The large wrought iron arch that bared the inn's name welcoming guests as they passed through it was set too far back to be seen until after the blacktop disappeared behind them. The only travelers in that area were either lost or looking for the old Europeanesque inn.

Coming from the east, it was 8.2 miles exactly from the last intersection. If you were coming from the west, it was almost impassable depending on the time of the year. The directions on the Ravenwood website clearly stated to detour to the south then get back on 116 on the east side unless you had a four wheel drive vehicle and were very well versed in how to operate it. They didn't own a tow truck, and search and rescue wasn't one of the many services offered by the concierge.

If you attempted that route and got lost, or worse, you'd have to call the county for help. You'd be at the mercy of a limited coverage area for cell phones. If something happened and you decided to wait it out in your car, you might as well begin writing your will.

The only people who traveled the twelve miles west of Ravenwood to the city of Appleton were the people who had grown up there. They were the people who knew the woods, who feared the creatures who dwelled there, but more importantly, they respected them. These were the people who had made friends with the woods for it were the trees who wouldn't let you leave, but even they would choose the long way whenever possible.

It may sound a bit unhinged, but the locals who share these stories do so with one purpose in mind. They pray some poor unsuspecting outsider never has to learn the truth about Ravenwood and the land that surrounds it the hard way.

Tourists have been found wandering in a different state hundreds of miles away claiming they blew a tire the night before on good old Route 116. They're always shocked to learn how far they were found from where they believed themselves to be. Their car is almost never located. These poor souls are never quite right again afterward. It's like whatever the trees did to them that night messed them up for good.

Wrecks that occur in these parts are even more unfortunate. It could take years for a shimmer off the metal of a car in the ravine to be discovered by a passerby. Human remains, if there are any, are almost always skeletal and scattered by wild animals. Since the pavement was first laid by the county, no one had survived a wreck on that twelve mile stretch between Appleton and Ravenwood. Because of that, it's labeled as the most dangerous road in the country.

Locals have their own theory. These unfortunate people

who find their car in a ravine, perhaps wrapped around the trunk of a tree are taken by the woods. A lifetime of servitude is the sentence for the damage they caused and the trespassing of which they're guilty.

The owners of the inn don't believe in any of the nonsense spewed by the townsfolk. That's what they'd have you believe anyway. They call it tall tales, but they don't mind how the stories grow and change until they're unrecognizable from the facts because it's good for business. Anyone with an internet connection can find Ravenwood with a quick search if they're looking for a good haunt, or they could stumble upon it in a social media post or article about the strange and unusual. If it weren't for the ghost hunters, the occult lovers, the morbid souls chasing the twisted and disturbed, Ravenwood would have ceased to be prosperous years ago.

Tourist season had always been summertime in these parts with a little carry over into the fall. The patchwork of colors on the forest floor created by the fallen leaves had drawn travelers to the east for as long as anyone could remember. Covered bridges scatter the country side giving a romantic charm to areas no sane soul would want to traverse once winter brings her blankets of white and sheets of ice to cover the land.

Luckily, it's not the sane souls that are drawn to Ravenwood like a supernatural pilgrimage. It's the daring and mystical that yearn to explore and discover the secrets held within these walls and the surrounding property. They make the trek regardless of the weather.

Accidents do happen, of course. People could succumb to curious fates wherever they roam. They needn't even wander for that matter for such horrible events to occur. The oddly high percentage of guests not leaving Ravenwood unscathed has not gone unnoticed, especially by the owners and the extremely high cost of insurance after years of mishaps. The addition of a waiver releasing the property from responsibility of any illness or injuries up to, and including death, a couple of decades ago only resulted in a skyrocketed appeal for adventure seekers.

The Weaver family has owned Ravenwood since it was built and owned the land it sits upon for generations before that. All around them, people were at the mercy of the trees, yet their family has a perfect record of remaining unharmed. While they maintain there's nothing more to these stories than small town gossip, the locals have their own version of proof consisting of one man.

Hank Miller is the oldest man in Appleton. At ninety-eight years old, he's seen more changes in a lifetime than any of these young'uns nowadays could wrap their head around. After the fire of '48, he's older than most of the buildings in town too and that includes Ravenwood. He was alive to see the trucks that hauled in the stone to rebuild it at least. Ravenwood isn't just an old inn buried off some state road in the middle of nowhere. It originated in Hungary.

When Joseph Weaver came home from the war, he brought a lot more back with him than anyone ever expected. Rozalia Margaret Weaver nee Pataki barely spoke a word of English and was very clearly near ready for childbirth. Joseph's pa didn't approve of his daughter in law, and as such, his mother wasn't too welcoming either. They did however impart him with a wedding gift: the family land near Appleton.

No one really knows what happened when Joseph went

into those woods to build a house for his growing family, not even old Hank. All he has are the stories his own parents passed down to him when he came along. Joseph and his wife went into the woods loaded up with supplies and tools enough to build a small house until they could afford better. They weren't seen again until no less than a decade later.

Both had long been feared dead, and a headstone for Joseph was erected in the family plot. There was ample fanfare for the memorial of their son, but his folks hadn't so much as written Rozalia's parents to break the sad news. The part that shocked the area the most when they wandered out of the trees just as casually as when they left was that neither of them looked a day older than when they ventured off together filled with hope for their future. Rozalia was just as pregnant as she ever was without any other children to show for it.

This was only the beginning of the bizarre origin of the Ravenwood mysteries. They left the woods to meet their shipment in a bay on the coast. Rozalia's family estate had been destroyed in the war, and they had the remnants of it sent over from Europe.

The entire state was abuzz with the news. There were more questions than there were answers, and the answers were really just anybody's best guesses. Where had they been all these years? Why did neither of them appear to have aged? What happened to the baby Rozalia was carrying when they disappeared all those years ago?

The one thing the young couple did better than creating mysteries was avoiding giving direct answers. They insisted they had only been gone a week, but didn't seem balked by the date either. It was as if the math was supposed to factor out correctly. One week in the woods was equal to a decade in Appleton.

Why go through the trouble and expense of moving the ruins of her family home across the ocean from Europe? Why not start afresh and build new? The biggest question of all was how had it been arranged.

The young couple had never mentioned it before their disappearance. If they truly believed they had only been gone a week and were planning on leaving to meet this shipment so soon, why go into the woods at all? If the arrangements had been made before their disappearance, why did it take ten years to arrive? It had to be such. How could they have made these arrangements without any trace of them having left the woods before now?

They were the hot topic of Appleton for a long time when Hank was a boy. Everywhere he went the adults were discussing the young couple of the woods. They wondered what was really coming over on this boat.

Surely it wasn't the remains of a home destroyed over ten years prior. Where had it been all this time? It would have been left in the elements collecting rain and snow, creating nests for rodents and who knows what other creatures. It would have been growing weeds from its cracks and covered in moss by now.

Then the shipment started to arrive. It strolled down the streets of Appleton on the bed of truck after truck, turning down Route 116 on a road that no God fearing man would ever dare to take. Dunberry Road wasn't paved, and with the rains, it wasn't safe for anyone. The trucks detoured around north and came down into Appleton. The people in town waved and smiled at the wonder of these large trucks grinding their way down Main Street. Once they were out of sight, they hung their heads and mumbled a prayer under their breath.

The Weavers never ceased to be the talk of the town, but the word going around was ever changing. Every truck that passed through was a sight to behold. Many in Appleton had never seen the new trucks revolutionizing the shipping industry until the Weavers had their deliveries.

A few were covered, but most were not. The only thing the people of the town were privy to lay their eyes on was stone. Rock after rock passed through the streets on the trailers of these large vehicles. It looked more akin to deliveries from a quarry than what they had pictured when dreaming up an image of a Hungarian home.

The drivers were tight lipped. The few who stopped to dine as they passed through would say nothing about their load or the young couple. It fueled the curious minds who created their own explanations when none were offered.

Young Joseph had declared he would rebuild his wife's family estate using as much of the original materials as possible. The spot they had chosen was set back close to a mile north of Route 116, twelve miles east of Appleton. The last shipment arrived just before the first snow fell in the fall of 1928. Each truck had safely voyaged from the small town of Appleton to the current location of Ravenwood to unload and back without a single incident. There wasn't so much as one flat tire. It was a record if there ever was one.

The old timers spent the winter arguing about the weather as was custom in those parts. Every snowfall led to a discussion about the years they could remember that saw it worse. There was one point everyone could agree on. It was the coldest winter anyone had known.

As it always did, the talk would wind its way back around to the Weavers. How were they faring? Where were they living until their home was built? Would it be another decade before anyone saw hide nor tail of them again?

Hank was only five years old that winter, but he could still vividly remember learning about the vast difference between the sexes. The men tolled on about the weather and had what amounted to a bit more than a passing fancy about the young couple. Most of their interest revolved around this Hungarian estate. What had it looked like? What would it look like when it was finished? Most importantly, how much did it cost to ship it here? There was even a friendly wager among a couple dozen or so of the men who gathered at the barber shop to weave their tales. That's if they were ever lucky enough to find out the final price.

When Hank was forced to tag along with his mom to her social events, he noticed the conversation was always a tad more sinister. The only thought concerning the Weavers that the women had on their minds was what became of Rozalia's baby. Not the one she was carrying now. Not the one she claimed to still be carrying for ten long years. They wanted to know what happened to the baby she was carrying when Joseph first brought his new bride to Appleton.

In every group, there was one lady who would offer a reasonable explanation. The baby had died from exposure. That's what it had to be. Humans were not meant to live in the wilderness like animals. As hard as it would be for an adult to survive, imagine the consequences of subjecting a poor, helpless babe to such circumstances. Losing a child is brutal. It changes a person. That's why they're claiming this new babe as the same. In each group, there was one, and only one lady who would come to what was best described as the defense of the Weavers'.

The rest of the group had a far more malicious explanation. Rozalia was Hungarian. What do we really know about her? Or her people? Did you see the dress she was wearing when she first arrived? Rags. She's probably a gypsy.

The collective assumption of the women in town was the original baby was sacrificed. Over ten years' time, a good number of babies could have been lost to her wicked ways. That's why they kept their youthful looks. Joseph Weaver, such a promising young lad, who would've made a good husband to any of the young ladies in Appleton, had brought a gypsy into their midst.

The spring of 1929 finally rolled around. The weather broke, and the snow melted. Still the Weavers remained in the woods. A group of men decided for the second time in their lives to go in search of them. Hank's dad was among them.

They took the long way around to venture up from the south knowing the risks they'd face if they took the more direct route. Joseph had said their home would be built eight miles west of Dunberry Road. The men agreed to drive not more than nine miles along Route 116. They would turn around long before reaching Appleton if they couldn't find the couple.

It was nearly three hours before his father returned home. It might not seem like enough time had passed to set off any alarms, but it had been sufficient for his mother to begin to pace the floor with worry. She'd walk from the kitchen where dinner was stewing to the front window to peer out and back. It was a path she'd been repeating for almost a half an hour when his dad's car pulled up to the house.

Whenever the phrase 'white as a ghost' gets tossed around, Hank's mind flashes the still picture image of his father when he walked in the house that day. The complexion of his skin matched the crisp whiteness of the shirt he wore. His mother grew frantic asking what had happened.

His father glanced at him and ushered her into the kitchen for privacy, but Hank, having just celebrated his sixth birthday and being of the firm belief that he was practically a man, stood flat against the wall bordering the kitchen in the front room next to the open doorway, hanging on every word that was said.

The group had found the Weavers with ease. Their home couldn't be missed. Even though it set back a mile off the road, it loomed through the tree tops. It was no Hungarian estate like any of them had imagined. It was a castle. It was a genuine, European castle in the backwoods of Massachusetts.

It was inexplicable. It was impossible. No one man could have accomplished such a feat over the course of one winter using rubble that had been shipped from Europe.

Every man, woman and child in Appleton had friends and family in all the small towns scattered throughout the countryside. No one had reported men being hired for work over the winter months, more shipments of materials, or strangers passing through who may have been in the area to work for Joseph. Talk of the Weavers had spread far and wide. Nothing that could make sense of what the group saw had made its way back to their town.

The castle was a sight to behold. It was beautiful inside

and out. The young couple readily welcomed them into their home and gave them the grand tour. Not only was the structure sound, but it was fully decorated. Every room was laid out in a blend of modern and antiquity. Rozalia seemed to have a story for each item from her family's history which she wistfully shared with her heavily accented and broken English.

The most astounding piece in the entire castle was a framed picture that adorned the downstairs hall. It was a photograph of the castle taken in Hungary before it was destroyed. It looked identical to the one the Weavers had built as if they had simply picked it up from its home in Europe and placed it down in the woods east of Appleton.

Of course, his mother was only concerned with the baby. She wanted to know if Rozalia was still pregnant. His father wasn't quick with an answer.

Hank's mother insisted with her questioning.

Eventually, his father went on to recant the last moments of their visit to Ravenwood with obvious disbelief of the validity of his own memory. Rozalia was as she'd ever been when they arrived. She appeared to be a woman ready to give birth at any time. After the tour, Joseph was chatting eagerly on about the build, about the difficulties, and about the techniques he used. His dad couldn't say any of the group would remember too much of what Joseph was telling them. They were still in awe of the place and too overwhelmed to pay close attention to the conversation.

Then Rozalia walked over, gently grabbed his arm, and told him it was time. The words were no sooner said when she clutched her protruding belly and screamed out in pain.

Eleven years to the day after returning home from the war,

Joseph ushered them out of the castle immediately. If she was still pregnant, she wouldn't be for long.

Chapter Two
Ravenwood Walking
Trail Rules

1. Trail hours are 8am to 4pm.
2. Stay on the marked paths.
3. No motorized or wheeled transport allowed.

i.e. motorbikes or skates

1. Handicapped tours are available with a guide including for those guests needing to use a wheelchair. Please register for one at the front desk.
2. No photography or video allowed of any kind. Prints are available for purchase in the lobby.
3. No food or drink except water.
4. If you have trash, keep it with you and use the nearest waste receptacle. Don't throw it down on, or especially off, the trail.
5. Surveillance cameras are in use for your safety.
6. No running. The trees view it as a threat.
7. Don't mock the woods.
8. Trail hours are subject to change daily due to staff discretion.

One of the biggest rules for the woods near Ravenwood was to stay on the marked paths. The rules were posted at the entrances of the trails and periodically throughout. Guests were also greeted to a list in the directory book inside their room.

There were two paths. The wider one was designed for joggers and dog walkers. It was fairly level grade and stayed near the grounds border. Imagine a running track with prettier scenery.

The path that drew in the most traffic was the one that wound its way through the trees showing some of the sights that had nurtured many of the wildest stories about the old inn. There was a tree growing through the middle of a car where the engine should be. The car had gone off the road during a heavy rain in the early 80's. Legend states the accident occurred less than a mile from Appleton, but the woods claimed the car and placed it where they wanted it. No one has an answer for what had happened to the engine.

Several trees could be seen from the path that had trunks resembling human like features. It's not just facial pareidolia. It looks like the trunks had been carved to look like people. Experts had been called out to examine them for a cable channel documentary and determined they were natural designs in the wood. Locals believe if those trees were chopped down, human remains would be found in every one of them. They think the trees took on the form of the life they claimed. It's also been said some have tried to see for themselves, but the blade of every saw and the head of every ax was broken on the first attempt. The trees won't let their secrets be discovered.

In 1992, a young guest went missing from the inn. Her

name was Marla Jackson, and she was only twenty-three years old. Everyone knew she wasn't really missing. She was claimed by the woods when she went exploring. Two years later, she was discovered sitting on a large rock less than fifty yards from the back of the inn. Marla was sitting upright with her hands in her lap. She was dead; her body petrified. It's rumored throughout the county her body is still being studied in a lab somewhere in Boston.

Miss Jackson's death sparked an intense and what was to be thorough investigation. Police essentially set up headquarters inside of Ravenwood. They wanted to interview everyone who worked at the inn around the time of the disappearance. There was even a local commercial that aired, asking the public to come forward with any information. It had been paid for by the poor woman's family.

Teams of officers set out canvassing the woods with a very structured and methodical system, hoping to find some piece of evidence that might remain. The shoes she had been wearing, her purse and a gold necklace with her birthstone pendant weren't with her body when she appeared out of the blue sitting on a rock like she had always been there. One officer broke his ankle and has always maintained, he felt something like a pair of hands push him into the ravine. Within an hour of rescuing him, two more officers were reported missing. They're still missing to this day. By nightfall, the case had been closed. Marla Jackson's death was ruled accidental. The two officers were declared dead also having succumbed to accidental injuries sustained in the line of duty. Even the locals were impressed the woods got to the police department too.

The number of TV programs that filmed on the property continued to grow. Ripley's featured them on several episodes. Ravenwood made Ripley's lists of the Weirdest of the Weird, Northeastern Novelties, Oddities of the Occult, and more. Ghost hunting teams came out of the woodwork to set up their equipment overnight and film at Ravenwood. None of them left disappointed. There was a price for everything, and if someone wanted to pay to come out and provide the inn with free publicity, the owners wouldn't turn it down.

Lorelei had walked the path through the trees every day since the first time her grandma shooed her out of the kitchen for being underfoot. There were seventy-seven steps from the entrance next to the rock where Marla had been found until the path came to an intersection. To the right was the recommended start of the trail although there was nothing stopping anyone from walking it backwards. Having the foot traffic flow in one direction prevented people accidentally stepping off the path as they passed each other. One footprint in the loose dirt might seem harmless anywhere else, but at Ravenwood, it couldn't be known what mood the trees would be in on any given day.

Directly in front of guests at the intersection was the second posting of the rules. The rules were posted every fifty feet from there until the path weaved its way back around to this exact spot. Overkill? Not at all given the number of guests who claimed to have not been made aware of them.

It took fifty-six steps to arrive at the first oddity. The number of steps it took had decreased over the years as Lorelei had grown. The counts wouldn't change again she would soon learn. At sixteen, her five foot three frame was the tallest she'd ever grow. She would know this because the lady of the woods was about to tell her so.

The trail weaved its way in and around the woods displaying its mysteries to the public. These weren't the actual secrets of the woods. The real wonders were still hidden and would remain that way. Lorelei continued on the trail paying no attention to the markers she had passed countless times before except one. She always paused at the contorted hazelnut tree.

It had twisted and turned as it grew while all the trees around it stayed straight in their course. That made blaming the irregularity of its shape on strong winds a weak argument. The imagery of it would be hard to dispute. It appeared to be a man in the process of falling to his knees. One branch took the form of an arm stretched behind him for support. Another branch looked like the other arm bent in front of his face for protection. The rest of the tree sprouted up from the top of his head, continuing to grow year after year. The look on his face, and the only souls who claimed not to see a face in the trunk of this tree were liars, was utter terror.

Lorelei had seen this tree enough to draw it from memory if she had the skill. Still, she hesitated every time she passed it. The one question she had no one could, or would as was probably the case, answer was about this tree. She had always wondered if Earl could still hear the guests who passed through.

Thirty-seven steps past Earl was the stairs taking you down into the shallowest end of the ravine. There was a more accessible trail, but only employees had the keys to open the gates. The woods weren't happy that another path had to be cleared through their home for those who were unable to go the direct route. While nothing had happened on that section of the trail yet, no one came back without the feeling of dread like they had barely escaped some awful fate. Most swore off ever returning to the woods, including the employees acting as guides. That's why all handicap tours had to be done by family.

The near end of the stairs and the sign posting the rules a few feet before them were her guidelines. She stood between them and waited. This was the only gap in security footage along the entire path. It gets mentioned from time to time, but no one had formed a compelling enough argument for the purchase of another camera and expense of man hours to install it for three feet of the trail. Where a guest disappeared off one screen, they'd reappear on the next. If they didn't, then it was a clear sign there was a problem.

Once in the safe zone as she liked to call it, she set the timer on her watch. It took the average guest around twenty minutes to get to this point. That was including the time they spent gawking at the sights along the way. If anyone had been monitoring the cameras which was unlikely given the season and lack of guests, staff would be here to search for her in less than ten. That's how long she'd wait before making her next move. The less her mother was aware that she knew, the better off they'd both be.

Each generation told their children less and less about Ravenwood. Some of the history may have been forgotten entirely, and some of it may have simply been forgotten to be included when passing it on to the next in line to inherit the castle and become the keeper of the woods. Lorelei's mother believed she could end it with her. If she didn't pass any of the so called secrets to her daughter, they would cease to exist.

It wouldn't work because the woods would still be there. The lives of those who entered could still be in danger. It didn't matter if you decided not to disclose anything to your children or not. That was your choice to seal their fate. Sending them to the woods unprepared amounted to no less than standing them before a firing squad except the woods wouldn't be as kind.

Once ten minutes had passed, Lorelei stepped off the path to the left of the sign, staying within the blind spot. When the cameras were first installed, this lack of coverage was done intentionally for the family to have secrecy. At some point, a new staff member noticed it and pointed it out, expecting high praise for a job well done. Her mom knew why this area wasn't under surveillance, but couldn't say as much. It would draw unwanted attention. A curious person could be more dangerous than an armed one. If any of their employees came out here to see why this area was so special, it would be hard telling how the trees would react.

There were twenty steps exactly behind the sign to the tall oak tree that was probably standing when the explorers from Europe first ventured this far inland. She circled it to the left and walked another eighty-nine steps until she reached the old staircase at the top of the ravine.

She wasn't sure when the last time the stairs had been redone, or if they ever had other than when the rail was added. When it was her turn to take over running the inn, it would be the first thing on her to do list. Calling them stairs was a polite nod to what they were supposed to resemble. Crumbling pieces of wood marked where the steps used to be, but the metal railing had survived. To access the well-worn walking path midway down the ravine, she had to walk down the steep incline next to the old staircase, holding on to the rail for support.

Great Yanyo Rose was the reason she had made friends with the woods. They had come to the clearing together many times for as long as she could remember. Yanyo Rose was probably bringing her out here before she could walk. It was through her that Lorelei learned everything her own mother didn't plan on ever teaching her.

The walking stick she used lay near the bottom. She picked it up and whispered thanks to the woods for letting her use it to aide her. Yanyo Rose had told her she only needed to do it once, but she insisted on doing it each time she came. Then she rubbed the top of the walking cane that had rested next to hers untouched for three years as she always did, saying hi to Yanyo Rose.

The railing was helpful and having stairs would be nice, but what was really needed was a better path along the wall of the ravine. Lorelei didn't depend on the walking stick too much. The only reason she had one was because she had wanted to be like her Great Yanyo.

It was about twenty yards from the stairs to where this side of the ravine leveled out. This was the only leg of the trip she didn't have a step count memorized because it varied every time she came. Her Yanyo Rose could casually walk along the ravine with her walking stick just as easily as she would walk across the kitchen floor to put the kettle on for tea. Lorelei walked it with one hand on the dirt wall to her right, her other arm outstretched for balance, and the hope that a root would reach out to save her if she slipped.

The ravine grew taller and taller above her head as she walked. At the end where it opened up, there was a sharp drop off well over a hundred yards above her that cut back toward the main road. The route she took might be more dangerous, but it was faster by a good hour, if not more, than taking the long way around.

This part of the property always looked more beautiful to her than the rest. She often wondered if it really was more picturesque, or if it was the knowledge that she was one of only a dozen or so who had seen this part of the land and lived to tell the tale that made it seem so appealing. It was something that could never be answered. She couldn't exactly bring a guest, not until she had a daughter of her own, and she wouldn't dare risk a photograph.

The trees wouldn't mind it. They enjoyed having their beauty appreciated, but that's not the only reason they would like it. If she showed an outsider a picture of this hidden, remote part of the woods, it would increase their curiosity. They would want to come see it for themselves. The trees loved having new visitors, but their blood would be on Lorelei's hands.

She walked her way through the maze of trees until she came to the small clearing. That's what she had always called this place because it was a circular area about twelve foot in diameter that was empty save for a small sapling growing in the bullseye middle of it. There were other bare spots all over throughout the property. This was the only area that was circular as far as she knew. Great Yanyo had called it the center.

When she stepped through the trees, she reached above her head and let her fingertips brush against the pendant that hung from a gold chain on the lowest branch. It was a sapphire, the birthstone of September. This was a habit forged almost to the point of superstition that she had begun when she was still young enough for Yanyo Rose to carry her. As she grew older, her Yanyo would lift her up until she was big enough to reach it by jumping. The first time she visited this place on her own after Yanyo Rose passed was the first time she was tall enough to reach it while keeping both feet on the ground. She had never been entirely sure the tree hadn't lowered its branch for her.

Once inside, she greeted the trees that formed the border by name. All trees have a name if you're lucky enough for them to share it with you. Lorelei took a couple steps and looked at the sapling with growing excitement. All around her she could hear the crunching and twisting of wood. The branches were bending and joining together to create a solid barrier.

She would be naïve to think they were protecting her. They were protecting their own. The sapling might appear younger than the towering trees that surrounded it, but as with many things in this area, looks were usually deceiving. It was both one of the oldest trees at Ravenwood and the last of its kind.

Lorelei took a deep breath and reached out to ever so gently touch one of its leaves. It had been explained to her what to do by Yanyo Rose. It was a story that had been told every time they came to this spot. This was her sixteenth birthday. It was time for her to meet the Lady of the Woods to discuss her future.

Chapter Three
The Proposal

Billy sped down Route 116 with one eye on the road, and one eye firmly fixated on getting a look down Heather's shirt. They could've gone anywhere for their two year dating anniversary, but she had heard about some castle in the middle of the countryside that intrigued her. An hour had passed since they left the restaurant, and he was trying to get them to the inn as quickly as possible. Tonight was going to be incredible. The ring was in his pocket, and it called to him like Poe's fictional heart. Every time he moved his arm, he worried the small box would fall out, giving away his secret plans.

"I wanna know..." he half mumbled, singing along to the radio.

"What?" Heather asked.

"I want you to show me," he belted out to her.

She smiled and looked away, shaking her head. It was almost as if she was trying to avoid directly looking at him during his serenade, she stared straight ahead while finishing off her soda before cracking the window far enough to toss it out. Her years of high school softball showed in her pitch. The can disappeared in the tree line before it hit the ground.

He continued to sing along to the song playing over the speakers. She acted shy, but he knew she loved it. The chorus was coming back around near the end of the song, and he was ready for the big finish. He took both eyes off the road for only a second when something ran out in front of them.

If Billy had survived the night, he would've sworn a beautiful woman with long flowing black hair appeared in the middle of the road from out of nowhere. She wasn't anywhere to be seen one moment then when he looked back, she was standing directly in his car's path.

Investigators would close the case as a bear attack even with only the trace amounts of evidence found near the wrecked Firebird. There was nothing to explain why the car had run off the road, or why the young couple hadn't made the turn on the lane up to Ravenwood a mile back if that's where they had been headed. There really wasn't enough to determine it was a bear, but something had to be blamed. An answer had to be given for what they found at the scene.

The tires locked up and the brakes screeched. Billy spun the wheel to the right in the opposite direction of where this woman was standing, and it quickly veered into the gravel along the edge of the road before diving into the ditch and coming to an abrupt halt. His head hit the steering wheel and the horn sounded.

He had no way to tell how long he had been out when his eyes opened. The horn was still blaring, and it continued even after he removed his head from the steering wheel. "Heather?" he mumbled out loud.

One headlight was busted, and the other glowed into the ditch. The entire dash was illuminated. The only thing that didn't appear to still work and be permanently on was the radio, including the clock. He tried the key, but it was jammed in place in the ignition. "Heather, are you alright?"

Billy tried to look to his right, but a sharp pain put a sudden end to his movement. He brought his hand up to rub the back of his neck, but it only increased the twinges he felt stabbing at him. "Heather!"

His heart raced with worry about her, anger over his car, fear that he may have hit someone, and the increase in pain he felt throughout his body. He turned his entire upper half to look at his girlfriend, but the passenger side was empty. Ignoring every ache he had no matter how great, he jumped around in the seat. He looked in the back and climbed up to look out the open passenger door. She was gone.

The driver side door wouldn't budge. He leaned against it with what little strength he had, but there was no give. When he drug his body across the center console to get out on Heather's side of the car, he felt the pain in his leg. It could've been his ankle. Wherever the pain originated, it was intense, and he wouldn't be able to make it far.

"Heather!" Billy yelled into the night. There was no sign of her. He gently touched his fingers to his head and felt the thick, sticky blood trail that went down his temple to below his ear. The ground around him spun like the realization of the head injury made his body react accordingly.

'How long was I out?' he worried.

Using the car for support, he hopped along to inspect the damage. It was totaled. The front passenger wheel was bent up under the engine. The front corner of the car was wedged back under the hood.

He stood up and looked around. The only light available to him was the one headlight primarily blocked by the ditch.

There wasn't much he could see. "Heather!" he tried again.

'Maybe she went for help.' Billy was all too mindful that thought was born out of hope. He had hope she wasn't badly injured. He also had hope help would be on its way soon.

With each movement, reminders were shouted about his injuries. It was a difficult task, but he made it to the trunk. There had to be a flashlight. He was almost positive he remembered throwing one in there some time ago. He felt his pants pockets then remembered the keys were still in the car, stuck in the ignition.

Billy turned to lean against the trunk. He needed to rest. He needed to sit down. He felt woozy and weak, but he didn't think he could make it back to the open passenger door. The angle of the car made it difficult to balance himself without putting too much weight on what had to be a broken leg.

"Heather!" He tried one more time, screaming as loud as he could before making the decision to move again. Nothing. The night would be eerily quiet if it wasn't for the sound of the horn. Not even a cricket responded. They were all probably scared away by the blasting monotone cry emanating from the car.

He was afraid to rest. A fear gripped him suddenly that if he sat down on the seat, if he allowed himself to relax, he might not wake up again. He had to stay awake until Heather returned or a random car happened upon him by chance. Instead of making his way back to the passenger side of the car, he braced himself to climb up the road side of the ditch to lean against the rear fender on the driver's side. It was much easier to rest against it, and he immediately saw why his door wouldn't open. It was barricaded by the sloping angle of the ditch that came down from the road.

There was no sign of a body. That was one good thing. He had half feared to see the wayward woman laying lifeless, pinned against the ditch by the Firebird's front bumper. No sign of the woman meant it had all been in his head. The wreck was entirely his fault and avoidable.

Minutes ticked by that felt like hours. A war raged in his mind. It was getting harder to remain upright as time went on. The longer he stayed here the more impossible it would be to find help if he were to venture off on his own. The inn couldn't be far. It had been maybe five minutes since they turned off of Dunberry. It couldn't have been more than ten. If that's where Heather had gone looking for help, it shouldn't be much longer.

'*Heather.*' He pat his jacket pocket again and felt the tiny box stashed inside. It was still there. He hadn't thought about the ring since he woke up alone in the car and briefly panicked it may have fallen out at some point. It was their anniversary which was why he chose tonight to propose, but he was no longer sure he would. He could try again, planning another romantic evening to set the mood.

He chuckled softly. "Although, asking her to marry me in the back of an ambulance would definitely be a story unlike anyone else's," he said to himself.

"What was that?" he asked the night air. He turned quickly to peer into the darkened woods behind him. In doing so, a pain rang out from his lower leg that brought him to the ground. He winced and groaned, rubbing his calf, trying to soothe the aftershocks that shot through his leg by comforting the area above where they originated.

He pulled himself upright using the trunk for support. His breathing had just returned to normal, and the pain almost subsided to the dull ache that had been there all along when he heard it again. Something was just out of sight in the woods not far from where he stood.

The rustling didn't sound like it came from some small, friendly creature with a fluffy tail that women like Heather cooed over. Whatever it was had to be much larger, and he had never wanted to see a deer emerge from the side of a country road late at night as much as he did in that moment. It never showed itself. It only continued to move along the underbrush, from one side to the other, traveling the length of the car plus a little more. It wanted Billy to know it was watching him and waiting.

'Stop being paranoid,' he told himself. *'It's nothing. You've dealt with far worse than this at the bar on any given weekend.'* The pep talk did nothing to stop him from taking a step down the ditch to have more coverage from the car. Even he saw the fault in his logic. The car wasn't going to protect him from anything except maybe rain. If there was something out there, he was a sitting duck with his leg.

That was it then. It was bad enough his sweet girlfriend was the one who had to head off into the night in search of a house to use the phone or a passing car who might be friendly enough to stop for her. He was convinced she probably thought he was dead, believing she would have tried frantically to wake him before leaving him and the car behind. With that hanging over his head, he wasn't about to be beaten into a puddle of fear by a hyperactive rabbit running through the woods.

Billy slowly limped his way around the car. He stood

hesitantly with his hand on the corner of the trunk. With his next step, he'd be on his own with nothing to balance against, and there was still a couple feet of ditch left to climb. He made it to the flat ground just outside the tree line and waited. Nothing had moved in the woods since he decided to face whatever it was instead of cowering behind the twisted block of metal that had earlier been his most prized possession.

Several feet to his left, a bush shook and several small branches littering the forest floor broke under the weight of something that had begun moving around. It renewed his determination, and he found the strength to pull himself out of the ditch on his own. The noise stopped, and he looked from one side to the other and back, waiting for it to decide to make itself known again.

There it was on his right. He hobbled forward until he was flush with the underbrush that made an entrance into the trees more difficult. When it moved again, it was several feet on his right. Billy went back and forth, following the sounds and beating around the growth, not paying attention to the scratches that were painting a road map on his hands.

It was as frustrating as it was distracting. His mind was empty of the worrying thoughts about Heather for the first time since coming to, and the blaring horn that still violated the night seemed more distant behind him. He followed his unknown tormentor back and forth several times until his pain couldn't be ignored any longer. "That's it!" he yelled into the nothingness.

Reaching near his head, he grabbed a low hanging sizable twig and twisted it off the branch. He whipped it into the bushes and the tall grass that grew around the trees, yelling like a crazy man. "Where are you?"

Several minutes into his outburst, he stopped to catch his breath and felt eyes falling heavily on him. He spun around quickly, too quickly, and fell down to his good knee. The road was still empty, but he had feared Heather had returned, watching him lose his temper and sanity to the underbrush that hid his visitor.

He crouched on the ground, nursing his leg and catching his breath. It was looking fairly tempting to him to just sink onto the earth and wait. If only he knew what he was waiting for or that there was something to be waiting on, he would do it in a heartbeat. Then he heard it.

From deeper into the woods, there was the unmistakable sound of laughter. It was a woman's voice. "Heather?"

It was difficult, but he managed to stand up, using his twig for support until it bent in two under his weight. There it was again. He couldn't be sure it was Heather's voice, but if it wasn't her, then who?

Scenes rapidly raced before his eyes in flashes like a camera taking pictures repeatedly in the night. There had been a woman in the road. He was sure of it. When he closed his eyes, he could see her. It wasn't a figment of his imagination after all. He was so confused, and his head pounded harder when he tried to remember it.

Without thinking, he ventured into the woods, calling after her. "Hello?"

He fought his way through the rough grown bushes which protected the trees from unwanted guests until he made it to the open floorplan of the forest. "Anybody there?"

The laughing returned again, and he followed it.

"Where are you?"

Something lashed diagonally across his face. It felt like a whip. Blood dripped from one cheek into his mouth just before the blood from his forehead on the other side of his head stung into his eye. He barely had time to react when something grabbed his ankles and pulled his feet out from underneath him. He fell back onto the ground with an echoing thud. The wind knocked out of his lungs, and he gasped desperately for air. It was the only reason he didn't cry out over the shooting waves of pain in his leg.

In the darkness, he saw shadows moving around him. Thin wisps of something circulated over him reminiscent of tentacles, but the air was filled with them. He rolled to his side and pulled himself to the edge of the woods. The underbrush was unforgiving as it clawed at him, ripping his jacket. He had almost made it. One hand was free and dug a grip into the earth to pull him forward.

A new stabbing pain shot through his leg as something unseen pierced his flesh. It went clear through, and he felt it wrap around him tightly. Then it pulled him back. He flew across the ground away from his car, and the sound of the horn that was his compass point drifted away until it could no longer be heard. He couldn't properly scream as his chin banged along every uneven surface and jutted out root along the way. The small box containing his future was in his jacket pocket underneath him, and it dug into his ribs.

Officer Friedrich stayed in the patrol car until the unmarked car parked near the Firebird, and the two detectives emerged. "What do we got?" the lead detective asked across the road as he got out, introducing himself and his partner.

"The car is registered to a William Langford, missing. The passenger is believed to be Heather Maddows. No purse or identification. She was a no show for her reservation at the inn last night," he added, nodding his head back toward the direction of Ravenwood.

"Missing, huh," the second detective said.

The lead detective turned to the woods and pulled his overcoat back with his hands, resting them on his hips. "Missing," he repeated. "Unfortunately, he'll probably stay that way."

He turned back to Friedrich and asked, "Who reported the accident?" while his partner began examining the car.

"A housekeeper saw the car when she was on her way in to work this morning."

The detective began making his way through the ditch toward the trees. Friedrich followed, but only to the edge of the road. "She disturb anything at the scene?" the detective asked.

"No. She said, and I quote." Friedrich flipped through the small notebook he pulled from his pocket. "She said, 'I won't step one foot on 116 past the Ravenwood lane if you paid me,' end quote."

Detective Maxwell laughed. "She's not from around here, is she?"

Friedrich wasn't sure what he meant by that. He'd been raised in this area and wasn't thrilled at the prospect of stepping off the road to join the two men.

Maxwell was almost to the tree line when he realized he was alone. He turned back at the patrol officer who was nervously shifting his weight in the gravel. "Don't tell me," he shook his head.

He took a couple steps toward the young officer and asked, "You were in Scouts right?"

"What?"

"Boy Scouts," Detective Maxwell clarified.

The officer scanned the branches of the trees with eyes that were certain something was prepared to pounce. "No," he finally said.

"It's simple. Don't hurt the trees."

Friedrich slowly moved his head in the direction of the detective, but his eyes didn't leave the woods. "Don't... Hurt..."

"The trees," Detective Maxwell said loudly, snapping his fingers to break the officer's gaze. "Mind your step, and don't disturb anything." He crooked his head toward the forest, silently ordering the officer to approach.

He paced the tree line, studying it. "Here," he said, squatting down.

Officer Friedrich walked up behind him. "What is it?"

Maxwell pointed to the earth. "See that? Drag marks. Looks like a piece of fabric there too," he pointed. He stood up and peered into the woods. "They go back a ways." He walked a few feet down then entered the trees, disappearing almost immediately.

It made Friedrich nervous. His heartbeat quickened and he glanced at Detective Lawson who was kneeling by the woman's body in the passenger seat.

"Got a shoe!" a voice boomed from the trees.

"What?" He looked in the direction of the voice, but no one was there.

Detective Maxwell stood up about ten feet away lifting a man's tennis shoe with his pen. He placed it back where he found it and whistled, clapping his hands and rubbing them together. He made his way carefully out of the trees back to the other two men.

"Bear attack," he announced.

The young officer stared at him. It was not a bear. "Bear attack?" he asked. Doubt dripped from his voice.

Maxwell nodded then saw the face of the young disbelieving officer. "Unless you disagree?" he asked. "If you want to conduct your own search, be my guest," he said, extending his hand toward the drag marks on the ground.

"N-no," he said anxiously. "It was a bear."

Detective Lawson laughed and stood up. "Leave the kid alone," he said, walking up the ditch to join them. "It's a shame. A young couple like this with their whole lives ahead of them? Just got engaged too."

"How do you know that?" Friedrich asked.

"See that rock on her finger? The jewelry box is on the floor by her feet," Lawson explained.

Maxwell shook his head. "That is a shame." He stared down the road toward the entrance to the lane at Ravenwood that could almost be seen in the morning light. "So close. I wonder how they missed their turn."

Chapter Four
Job Interview

The lane to Ravenwood was every bit of the creepy she had imagined plus a lot more. The trees were thick on either side, and the branches leaned toward each other over the lane giving the feeling of being inside a tunnel. The sun was almost completely blocked which made it seem like dusk even though the morning was still young. There was a metal arch that bared the inn's name. At one time, it may have been an inviting sight, but it was now overgrown with vines on the sides, leaned at an awkward angle, and the covers for the side lights had busted.

"Relax," her brother said. It was practically the only word that had come out of his mouth since they left home that morning.

Alice took a deep breath, but there was nothing that could calm her as they inched closer to the inn that now loomed ahead of them. She recognized it from the many pictures she had seen over the years, but it didn't look anything like she expected. The photographs used in advertisements showed a beautiful castle set in an exquisite countryside. What lay before her looked like a rundown manor long forgotten in the wilds of Europe. Even the pictures her brother had taken since he started working for the Weaver family over a year ago looked a lot brighter and newer than the reality did.

He pulled into the lot on the side of the inn and continued around to the far end before parking. This was something she had sworn she'd never do. The last place on earth she wanted to work was Ravenwood. That's how most people in the area felt except for the weirdos who found the place cool. For many of them, there wasn't much choice.

Ravenwood would employ anybody. That's not to say they only hired people with poor work history, drug habits, and arrest records. No, anyone could work there. It didn't matter your age, gender, race, sex, schooling, past, or anything. There was no rhyme or reason to it. A person with a decade of housekeeping experience would be turned down over someone with a degree in Chemistry for the same job. It had nothing to do with pay either. They generously paid all their employees to keep them around because a sane person had to have some kind of motivation to deal with the crazy goings on her brother hinted about.

"You'll be fine," Bobby said for the seventh time. "Take deep breaths and relax." He looked at her like he was awaiting a response.

She nodded at him and took a deep breath. It was his day off, but he drove her for the interview. Their parents had insisted on it, not that he drove her, but that she applied here.

After Frank hit her, her life was turned upside down. She wanted to leave him, but didn't have the money to get her own place. They both worked, but he spent her pay as quickly as she could earn it. Everyone tried to warn her about the situation she was in, but she wouldn't listen. She was too in love to hear one bad word about her husband.

They had a small apartment in the city and one car between

them. Frank rarely let her use it. She took the bus to work and didn't mind too much. Even on his days off, she took the bus because he always needed the car for something. Eventually, she stopped asking.

If you looked at their finances on paper, they should've had plenty of income with some to spare to splurge or save. There was never anything left. They always lived paycheck to paycheck. The few times she got the courage to ask him about it he found ways to explain how it was spent that made sense to her even if she couldn't track where the money went.

The night he hit her she grabbed her jacket and purse then walked out without a second thought. As she walked, doubt crept into her mind. She didn't have any close friends anymore. The ones she used to have drifted apart from her years ago. The only place that would readily accept her was her parents. That was a call she swore she'd never make. The last thing she wanted to hear was, 'I told you so.'

It was getting late, so she headed to a mom and pop motel to get a room. Her mom had always told her things would look better in the morning, and she prayed that was true this time. She'd get a room and a good night's sleep. Maybe an answer would come to her tomorrow that she wasn't seeing tonight.

The front desk was located in a small room that couldn't fit more than three normal sized people. The bug zapper outside was loud and could be heard buzzing even with the door shut. Inside, one of the fluorescent lights was about to go out and blinked on and off above her. From where she stood, she could see the green neon of the motel sign displaying they had a 'VANCY' as two of the letters weren't lit. There was a sign on the counter announcing the desk hours.

Alice checked her watch, and her heart skipped a beat. It was after eleven. Time had been lost on her while she had walked. According to the sign, desk hours ended at nine. There was a number to call for late night check-ins.

She hesitated and thought about leaving. The hours she spent walking around the city was starting to speak to her through her sore leg muscles, and the realization of how late it was made her doubly worn out and tired. It was too far to walk home, not that she had an inclination to go there anyway.

The phone had been set on the counter, and she dialed the number. The man who answered had a gruff voice, and he sounded annoyed. "May I help you," he barked.

"Yes, I need a room," she told him.

"Call back in the morning for reservations," he said.

Afraid he was about to hang up, she quickly said, "No, I'm here. At the desk. I need a room tonight."

There was a long groan before he said, "One minute."

It took closer to fifteen before he came through the door marked 'Office' behind the desk. When the door opened, Alice could see a hideabed couch that was pulled out. The bedding was in disarray. The man was dressed casually, and his hair was disheveled. If he hadn't been asleep when she called, he had definitely been laying down, attempting to get some rest.

They went through the process of getting her checked in. He had her sign the guest book and took information off her ID. "That'll be $33.27," he told her.

'Outrageous,' she thought. For that price, the room had better be pristine and not smell musty and of mildew like most of these small joints did. Alice dug through her purse to find her small makeup compact that stashed her emergency money.

It was hard to do, but she sometimes managed to tuck away five dollars here and there without Frank knowing about it. When she opened it, there was nothing inside except the mirror.

Her heart stopped and her stomach sank. *'No,'* she thought. There was no way Frank had known about the money and never said anything. So he just happened to find it right before this big fight? *'No!'* she thought again, rifling through her purse in the hopes the money had fallen out of the compact. That was why he started the fight over what she made for dinner. This was actually what made him so mad tonight.

When she looked up at the man behind the counter, her face said everything, and he reacted accordingly. He took the guest ledger down from the counter and scratched out her name. Then he hung the room key he was about to hand her back on the small hook on the wall.

"I'm so sorry," she said.

"Have a good night." He disappeared through the office door without a care to hear her apology.

The only option left to her was to call home. It was the first thing that had really upset her all night. The punch to her face hurt physically. Even though it signified the end of her marriage, it didn't make her cry. That said a lot about her marriage as far as she was concerned. She was filled with worry and anxiety over what her next move was going to be, but it didn't break her. The thought of calling home had her in tears before she made it to the pay phone.

She had thought about using the phone at the motel, but she was too afraid the burly man may emerge from the office again. He was already angry with her, and she didn't want to make the situation worse.

Her parents would've gone to bed hours ago. Now she'd be waking them up with a collect call, pleading with her dad to drive into the city to pick her up. It was tempting to go home to Frank. After the call, she sat on a parking block near the motel front desk for over an hour waiting on her dad. There wasn't a lot of traffic, but when a car did pass, she toyed with the frayed cuff of her bell bottoms not wanting to meet anybody's stare.

That was three weeks ago. Frank got her fired from her retail job by calling to complain about her and having his friends do the same. She knew it was him, but she couldn't prove it. No one was hiring in the small wisp of a town where her family lived. There were two gas stations and a restaurant. That was the bulk of it for work. Alice had wanted to use her mom's car to find a job in the city. It was older, but it still had some life left. Her mom didn't use it much, and she hoped they could agree to the arrangement until she saved enough cash to buy a used car.

They didn't and not because they were worried about the wear and tear either. Her mom didn't want to give up her freedom. Instead, they told her to apply at Ravenwood. If she didn't get the job there, her mom would chauffeur her to interviews in the city as well as take her to and from work until she had her own wheels. She had put up a fight about it for as long as she could. Any job, regardless of how hard or nasty, would be better than that. To make it worse, she knew she'd be hired because of her brother. He insisted that wouldn't make a difference, that they never hired based on staff recommendations, but she wasn't sure she believed him.

Bobby told her to relax again when she got out of the car, but it was hopeless. The inside of the castle would have set her nerves on edge again if she had managed to do as he said. It looked like one might expect, old and reminiscent of another era. There was a shroud of something that hung thick in the air. Without hearing a single story about the inn, she would have sensed there was more than meets the eye. It made her skin crawl, and she felt like she was being watched by more than one unseen voyeur.

The job interview didn't last long. It was a few minutes of basic questions and going over her application then they were done. Alice was relieved. When Mrs. Weaver walked into the room behind her, Alice's heartrate quickened, unsure if the noises were being made by someone real. Then Mrs. Weaver dropped her notebook and pen on the desk. The sound made Alice jump so hard she knocked her chair over. She was too worked up to form coherent answers to most of the questions and had to attempt her responses several times. This wasn't her first rodeo, and she knew she hadn't impressed Mrs. Rosemary Weaver. The strange presence inside the walls of the inn closed around her as she left almost making her run at full speed for the side door that led to where her brother was waiting for her.

Once outside, she was fine. No, she was relieved. It was over, and there was no chance they'd be calling to offer her the position of second shift desk clerk. She was far from fine and wouldn't be until they were down the road with the inn long behind them.

"How'd it go?" Bobby asked.

She shook her head and rested it on the seatback looking up at the headliner of the car. There was a tear near the passenger winder she had never noticed until now. "That depends on how you look at it."

He pulled out of the parking spot and steered the car out onto the lane. "How's that?"

"I bombed it which means I won't get the job. As far as I'm concerned, it went perfectly, and I didn't even have to try to tank."

They made it to the end of the lane, and he pulled the car out onto 116 heading toward Dunberry Road. "You didn't relax then?"

So many things about her brother amazed her like how he could work at the most spooky, haunted, cursed, and frightening place in the state if not the country without batting an eye. They were total opposites if he thought she could step foot on that property without her blood pressure shooting through the roof and feeling nauseous from fear. "Hardly," she said with a laugh. It was easier to breathe once Ravenwood was in the rear view, and she knew it wasn't a coincidence.

He looked over at her before making the turn onto Dunberry. "You should've relaxed."

It was like it was the only word in his vocabulary. "Well, I'm glad I didn't. They could probably sense how terrified I was the moment I walked through the door."

"That's what I was afraid of happening."

She shook her head. "If I had relaxed, the interview probably would've gone better. I don't want that job, Bobby."

"I know," he said quietly.

For the life of her, she couldn't figure out why he was acting that way. No one actually wanted to work at Ravenwood. They applied there out of desperation. From time to time, some kook would come to the area who was gung ho about ghosts, demons, and who knows what else. They wanted to get a job at the inn because they were a few cards short of a full deck. The inn never hired them. At least the family that owned it had some sense in doing that. Everyone who worked out there went to that place out of desperation, but they somehow ended up liking it. They might talk about the place like it scared the wits out of them, but they wouldn't leave. Bobby had always defended it by saying the pay and benefits were amazing.

'Shoot,' she thought. *'That's what he's worried about.'* They had to know she was his sister. He didn't want her reflecting poorly on him.

"I'm sorry, Bobby," she said. "I hope they don't give you a hard time over me being terrified."

He shook his head then flashed a smile at her. "It's fine. What will you do if they offer you the job?"

Alice laughed out loud at the question. "They won't," she said. There wasn't the slightest chance they'd consider her for the front desk.

"But what if they do?" he asked again.

She rolled her eyes at her younger brother. "*If* they do, I'll turn it down. I'm sorry, but I don't know how you do it."

"What about mom?"

Both of their parents would be angry if they found out she turned down a job offer. They loved their children, but money was already tight before Alice came back home. "I just won't tell her. I'll say they hired someone else, or that I never heard back from them."

He nodded slowly while chewing his cheek. The rest of the drive was silent, and she couldn't shake the feeling there was something he wasn't telling her.

When they walked through the front door, their mom

yelled out from the kitchen. "You're back!" Her voice told them she was in a good mood. She typically was, but this was something more.

She walked out of the kitchen smiling from ear to ear. "You got it!"

"What?" Alice asked confused.

"The job," her mom said. She walked over and took Alice's hands, shaking them excitedly. "Ravenwood just called and said the position was yours! They want you to start on Monday."

Their mom headed back to the kitchen. "You need to call them back," she added before disappearing.

The room started to spin around her, and Alice put her hand on the arm of the sofa for support. This couldn't be happening. *'And mom knew!'* There had to be a way to get out of it, but nothing was coming to her. She looked at Bobby for help.

"I was afraid of this," he said.

Before she could ask him what he meant, their mom was back. "To celebrate, I'm making your favorite for dinner. Spaghetti and meatballs!" she sang out.

Alice closed her eyes and rubbed her temples with her free hand. She hated spaghetti. It wasn't her favorite; it was their dads. Their mom meant well, but she was always confusing her children. She considered dad to be the biggest of her children she had to look after.

"I told you to relax," Bobby said.

She popped one eye open and glared at him. Why did he keep saying that as if it had anything to do with the hell she had just walked into?

"Sure," she said sarcastically. "Because maybe then they'd

have offered me the job on the spot instead of leaving a message with mom?"

"That's not how it works," he said.

Alice sat on the sofa bent over with her elbows on her knees. Her head was held up by her hands. "This can't be happening," she moaned softly.

Bobby was becoming quite annoying by this point. "I tried to help."

"How?" she asked, lifting her head to look at him so fast she felt something pull on the right side. She rubbed at her neck, and told him, "The only thing you've done all day is tell me to relax. Like that was even possible!"

He shifted his weight nervously and looked around like he was afraid someone might hear what he was about to say. "They feed off your fear."

A shudder went through Alice. What he said and the somber tone he used was the creepiest thing she'd ever witnessed her brother do.

"Your insecurities. Your self-doubt. All of it. That's what they want. It's what they need, and they can sense when someone shows up overflowing with it."

She had a feeling she would regret it, but she asked anyway. "Who's they?"

"The woods," he said, looking at her like she should already know.

"Oh, come on, Bobby!" She dropped her arms and dangled them to the floor. From the kitchen, their mom was humming as she banged pots and pans around to start cooking their dinner. She'd get fired. That's what she would do. She would find a way to get fired because if she quit, there'd be the devil to pay at home.

"That's why I told you to relax," he informed her.

She threw her arms in the air. "Yeah, you said to relax. Why didn't you just say the trees will give you the job based on your anxiety if you don't calm down if that's what you meant?"

He waved her off and took a couple steps back. "They don't want their secrets told."

She stared at him for several long moments in utter disbelief at the words her brother was saying. "You don't seriously believe all that nonsense, do you?" she finally asked.

"Don't you?"

"No," she said. There was no way a haunted forest of sorts existed anywhere, let alone less than twenty miles from their front door. It was superstitions and exaggerated stories that had been handed down for decades. Each new generation added their own urban legend about Ravenwood to the mix. That's what the logical part of her brain tried to convince her was the case.

Bobby started to leave, heading down the hall to his room, but he stopped at the doorway. Without turning back, he asked, "Then why were you so afraid to go there?"

Alice didn't answer him. She couldn't. She didn't believe in ghosts or things that go bump in the night, or rather, she didn't want to believe in them. When it came to Ravenwood, she couldn't help but wonder how much of it, if any of it, was true.

Chapter Five
It's Not My Fault

Reed barreled down Route 116 away from Appleton, checking his rear view and surprised to find he was still alone on the road. His exit wasn't as clean as he had hoped. Everything had gone wrong, so the roadblocks he encountered leaving town didn't surprise him. He hadn't expected the town's bicentennial celebration to kick off today with a parade down Main Street. Normally, he'd take a busier route where he could blend, get lost in the traffic, but it had only been his green AMC on the road since leaving Appleton behind him.

The oldies station on the radio played quietly, but the background noise was doing little to calm his nerves. "All the little birds on Jaybird Street," he half sung, before taking a swig from his Pabst. "Go tweet, tweet, tweet."

There was a small opening in the woods on his left that he barely caught sight of as he raced past. He screeched the car to a hault and backed up for a closer look. The ditch was virtually nonexistent here, so it would be fairly level to drive into it. The real risk was what may be on the ground that he can't see. A flat tire out in these parts was the last thing he needed to finish the day.

"Flappin' their wings, singing go bird go," he sang, driving off the road into the cover of the trees. He drove far enough into the woods to make it difficult to see his car from the highway. He put it in park, killing the engine, and downed the rest of his beer. "They started going steady and bless my soul, he out-bopped the buzzard and the oriole," he continued to sing even without the radio accompanying him.

He got out and eyed the road. The car could still be noticed, and it was hours till sundown. There was no end to the camouflage options around him. He opened his trunk and pulled out a hunting knife. Within minutes, he had a pile of branches to cover the back of his car, hiding it from view. He tossed the knife back in the trunk and opened a carton of Lucky Strikes, removing one pack before closing the trunk. The branches took several minutes to get them laid out strategically over the small Gremlin. When he finished, he walked toward the road, turning back to examine his work. It stuck out like a sore thumb for someone who was just standing around, but coming down the highway at a high speed, it wouldn't be noticed near as easily.

Reed packed the cigarettes against his palm then ripped off the cellophane top. He put one between his lips and lit it, thinking about how sloppy he had been. He hadn't seen the kid, and that made all the difference. The boy couldn't have been more than 8 or 9 years old and had been in the back of the convenience store. The kid was short enough that Reed couldn't see him over the tops of the rows. As he walked through the store, the kid must have gone from one aisle to another that he had previously checked without him noticing.

Everything was going smoothly until the kid screamed. It made him lose his focus when he turned to see the little boy standing there, shaking with fear. When he turned back, the clerk was reaching under the counter. It wasn't his fault. If the kid hadn't screamed, if the clerk hadn't decided he would try to be a hero, the rest of it wouldn't have happened.

Pictures rotated through his mind like frames of a movie. He pinched the bridge of his nose between his thumb and index finger and squeezed his eyes shut, trying to focus on something, on anything other than the convenience store. *'It wasn't my fault,'* he repeated to himself.

He concentrated on controlling his breathing while imagining a beach. It wasn't any beach he had ever been to before, but it was one he planned on visiting often in the future. He focused on the beach until the sound of sizzling and a whiff of singed hair caught his attention. He moved the hand holding his cigarette away from his face, and he felt his hair to survey the damage with his free hand while taking another drag.

In his thirty-seven years, he had never had anything go south this fast or this bad. There had been numerous close calls, too many to count. That's why he never stayed in one place too long to avoid getting caught. He had even been picked up and charged a couple times for writing bad checks and pick pocketing. The warrants bearing his name were still valid out in Arizona and Colorado. That's why he decided to try his luck out east. Well, that and Grace.

'It always comes down to a woman, doesn't it?' he thought. They can make or break you.

Reed had picked her up on the side of the road near Davenport after her car broke down. He drove her into the city and helped her find a garage who towed the Riviera in right away. They had lunch, and he sprung for her motel room since her car wouldn't be ready until the morning. Grace had told him she could cover it, but he insisted because he hoped to stay with her for the night. And, what a night it was.

Women and crime were the only two areas where he had ever excelled. Women had always come easy for him. The only thing easier than finding a woman was letting them go until he met Grace. When he kissed her cheek as they said goodbye the next morning, she slipped a piece of paper with her phone number on it in his hand, telling him to look her up if he was ever in Boston. He stuck the paper in his pocket right next to the two fifty's he had taken out of her purse while she was in the shower. The scrap of paper would later make its way to his wallet where it would stay until he finally thought to call her several weeks later.

Grace was different. She took what he was willing to give and never asked him for more. She didn't demand titles or definitions of what was developing between them. It was also the first time he had met a woman who would call him out on the line of bull he fed to her. The frequency of the phone calls increased until they talked nearly every night. When the day rolled around she told him she loved him, it made him smile instead of flee.

Reed knew she deserved better than he could ever offer. He wasn't exactly relationship material. There really wasn't anything he could do for her except break her heart. He had never earned an honest day's wage in his life, and he could definitely never be faithful. The first time he told Grace he loved her he had said it with another woman in his bed. She was a cute red-headed waitress he met an hour earlier and entertained for a few days before moving on.

Somehow he convinced himself he could make it work. He'd travel to Boston, to Grace. There wasn't much he was qualified to do to make a legitimate living except possibly for mechanics. He did know his way around a carburetor.

He could see it all working out in his mind. As he made the trek east from Lansing, his gut was saying otherwise. During the trip, he had knocked off several gas stations even though he had the funds to make it to Grace before he left Michigan. He didn't want to show up empty handed. Grace wasn't some mark that he intended to be his next target.

The closer he got to Boston the gnawing feeling in the pit of his stomach grew, screaming at him that he was making a mistake. All this time he thought it was nerves from the idea of settling down with a woman. Turns out his gut was trying to tell him that his luck had run out.

Reed flicked his still burning cigarette into the woods. It was a little odd how everything flipped. When he left the boy lying on the floor of the convenience store, knowing he was facing the worst trouble he had ever been in if he were caught, the feeling of dread he'd had for almost two weeks vanished. His mind which had been completely calm, day dreaming about playing house, was now a cluttered mess, and it was hard for him to grasp a single thought out of the mix for longer than a few seconds.

The boy had screamed which caught him by surprise, and he turned around to see where the high pitched noise originated. What obviously had to be a happy day had taken a much darker twist when he saw Reed pull the gun. The poor thing stood there with a balloon tied to his left wrist, and in his other hand, he was holding the small bag of chips he was about to buy before returning to his family along the side of the road to watch the parade. A few drips coming off of the cuff of his pants quickly turned into a pale yellow puddle between his legs on the tile floor.

That distraction kept his attention off the clerk for no longer than two seconds, but it was long enough. When Reed whipped his head back to the employee he had just ordered to pile all the cartons of Lucky Strikes on the counter, it was his worst fear. The cigarettes were there, but the employee was reaching beneath them, reaching under the counter for what Reed realized had to be a gun.

This was the one thing he dreaded in his line of work. It had always been a matter of time. There had been too many easy in and out jobs. The odds were stacked against him and had been for a long time. He had long been aware one of these times it would come to this. The fear wasn't over being shot or worse, killed. He honestly had never been sure if he would have it in him to pull the trigger. That's what woke him up at half past three in the morning in a cold sweat. It was the angst he would hesitate, and that would be his downfall.

But Reed didn't hesitate. As soon as he saw the clerk's movement, he fired. The guy behind the counter had a fresh out of high school look to him, but when he recoiled from the bullet and fell to the floor, his face appeared no older than the child standing in a puddle of his own urine nearby.

The marching band was making its way down the street on the side of the store. The percussion section was still a block away, and the sounds of the drums were a little faint to Reed's ears. Outside, the band and the cheers of the town folk in attendance were the only silencer he needed.

Reed had to move fast. He opened the army duffle he had swiped at a laundromat so long ago he couldn't remember what state he was in, but he could remember the eyes of the legless Vet in a wheelchair who yelled after him, wheeling as fast as he could. He held it open and pushed the cartons off the counter into it, unable to bring himself to look at the clerk's body.

There was another scream behind him, and he looked just in time to see the little boy's feet come out from under him and fly up in the air. The boy came down hard on his back, and his head bounced off the floor. He had tried to make a run for it while Reed wasn't looking, but slipped in his own mess.

He rushed to the boy's side, but didn't see any blood. "Are you alright, kid?" he asked.

The boy nodded while tears washed his face, and his snot formed bubbles from his nose with every exhale. Reed wasn't sure what to do, but he had to get out of there. The prevailing thought was he needed to save his own skin. He helped the boy to his feet and tried to assure him everything would be fine. "Can you count to 100?" he asked.

A low whine that grew into a wail was the only verbal response, but the kid nodded again.

"Alright, then. Listen. When I leave, count to 100 then go find your mom. You'll be fine," he said, waiting for the boy to acknowledge that he understood.

Distractions were the enemy. He began living on the streets, committing petty theft to survive when he ran away his junior year of high school. Everything evolved from there, and he had been successful because he kept a sharp head, staying on task until he was in the clear.

While he was tending to the kid, he didn't see the clerk

stagger to his feet behind the counter. The bullet which Reed assumed hit where he aimed and killed the young man had only wounded him, making it difficult to steady the gun with his dominant arm injured. Neither he nor the boy noticed the young man had raised the gun at Reed until he pulled the trigger.

The sound of the shot stunned Reed, and time moved in slow motion. He turned toward the clerk expecting the feel of liquid fire to pour through him as the bullet ripped into him. He fired back, hitting the clerk in the chest three times.

That's when he saw the kid laying on the floor once more. Blood poured from his neck, and the fear in his eyes faded along with any spark of life those eyes once held. Reed wanted to get help, but he knew it would be too late. The pool of blood continued to spread and the spray that shot from his neck over the candy on display at the front of the counter began to weaken. There wouldn't be enough time to save him.

Reed grabbed his bag and hit the no sale button on the register. The drawer opened, and he grabbed all the cash, throwing the bills on top of the cigarettes. This time he did look at the clerk, and he fired one more shot into his head. It wasn't to make sure he was dead because he didn't want him alerting anyone to come for Reed. It was for the kid who didn't deserve to spend his last moments having his blood mix with his urine on the floor of a convenience store all alone.

He lit another cigarette, and movement caught his attention. This was new. There still wasn't a car to be seen, but a woman was walking along the edge of 116 coming from the direction he had just left. She was quite a vision, stunning from head to toe, and he knew he hadn't missed her on his drive.

There hadn't been any houses or side roads along the way, so she had to have been in the woods herself which made him all the more intrigued.

When she was about ten feet away, he wandered out to the road in front of her. "Hey," he greeted.

She didn't say anything, but stopped when she reached him.

"Where are you headed?" he asked, like he had any knowledge of the local geography.

"Wheaton," she told him.

"Where's that?"

"It's a ways south on Dunberry," she said.

If anyone was after him, they'd have been here by now. "Want a ride?"

The woman curiously raised an eyebrow at him. There wasn't a car in sight.

He went back to where he stashed his Gremlin and began uncovering it. His mind tried to find a believable reason for why he had hid it in case she asked about it, but she never did. Once he had it on the road, she climbed in the passenger seat. They headed for Dunberry, putting more distance between him and Appleton.

"Want some music?" he asked, turning the radio on. Static hissed out of the speakers, and he tried tuning in a different station. It was no use. The reception was terrible the further away from town he drove and nothing was coming in. He flipped it off and leaned back stretching his arm to the side and resting his hand on the back of her seat. He hoped she'd mistake the bulge from the gun shoved down the front of his pants for something else.

"Headed home?" he asked.

"No, I have some business to take care of," she said.

"That's too bad."

The woman smiled at him, and there was something mischievous in the look on her face. "Why? Would you like to go home with me?"

"Mmm," he inhaled deeply. "Don't you know it."

"That can be arranged."

"Really?" he asked.

The woman leaned closer to him. "Yes, if you'd like. I'll take you home with me. All you have to do is say the word."

"What word?"

"The magic word, of course."

"Please," he said, rolling his eyes.

Moving quicker than he could react, she grabbed the steering wheel and whipped it sharply to the left. His feet wouldn't move on command. Reed tried to move his foot to the brake, but all it did was press the gas pedal down to the floor. He fought her for control of the steering wheel and was surprised by her strength.

The car went off the road and back into the woods. She maneuvered it expertly, weaving around trees, fallen logs and large boulder style rocks until the car slammed into the trunk of a tree at least three feet wide. It hit hard enough the driver's door popped open. The windshield shattered either from impact or from Reed's body flying across the hood. Not even the trunk of the tree stopped his movement.

"Honey, we're home," the lady said, getting out of the car.

An anonymous tip came in to the police station telling the department where Reed's car could be safely found. The crackling and popping on the line made it difficult to hear the voice of the woman who called. The unit dispatched to search the area found a trail of unopened packs of cigarettes leading them straight to the green AMC.

The trunk was open with the rest of the loot inside. The $87 and all ten cartons of Lucky Strikes taken from the convenience store in Appleton had been recovered except for one pack of cigarettes. The gun laying on the front seat matched the gun used in the robbery homicide. The experts who would later examine the car determined there was no way Reed survived the wreck. His body was never found, but the face like features etched in the trunk of the tree his car had hit matched the description of their suspect.

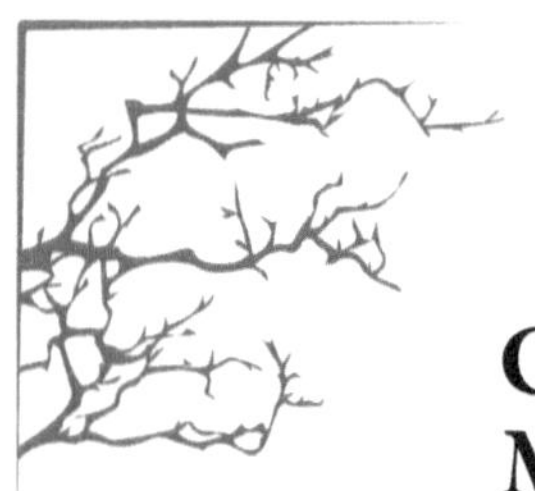

Chapter Six
Marco Polo

Craig and the boys were only looking to have a little fun. Growing up forty miles north of Ravenwood, they had all heard the stories. Every child had their pants scared off of them with the tales of the haunted woods that surrounded the old Hungarian castle. As they grew older, they saw the stories for what they were - stories. Tales that had been woven into camp fire ritual, and they did their part by passing them on to the next generation, adding their own twists and flare as they did.

It was a simple plan. One that would've guaranteed a few laughs at the end of the night except they overlooked one small detail. They never stopped to consider the stories might have some element of truth to them. If they had, they would've never entered the woods that night.

The three friends loaded up the old Monte Carlo SS with their girlfriends for a night in the city. That's how everyone in the area referred to Appleton, but by actual city standards, it was barely a large town. It was the closest place around for entertainment. They stayed out a little too late intentionally and made the decision to drive Route 116 to Dunberry instead of taking the long way around to get back home since two of the girls had a strict curfew. None of them let on it had all been premeditated.

Everything was unfolding as they hoped. Their girlfriends were uneasy, bordering on fright. They kept their objections to themselves aside from asking if they were sure it was the best option, but their nonverbal cues spoke volumes. As soon as Craig suggested 116, they crossed their arms instinctively over their bodies as a sign of discomfort and distress. The girls shifted around nervously and moved just enough to stand ever so slightly behind their boyfriends. It was clear they didn't want to risk that route, and they were responding even better than any of their mischievous boyfriends had hoped.

In the end, only five teenagers climbed into the car in the bowling alley parking lot. Aaron's girlfriend Tonya chose to stay behind and call her older brother for a ride home. She'd rather face the anger of her father for being late and have to devise a story of her own for why she needed a ride then join the rest of them on that road.

Aaron did his best to convince her to come along. He can't be faulted for that because he gave it his all, pulling out all the stops. Not only couldn't he convince her to stay with him, but they almost lost the other girls too. When she suggested that any of them could stay and ride with her, Craig unconsciously held his breath until the girls responded. He had already seen it in their eyes. They were considering it even before she offered. The moment Tonya said she wasn't going their eyes lit up. None of them had felt like they had an option, but here it was. They didn't have to face their childhood terrors anymore if that's what they chose.

He was confident his girlfriend Michelle would stay with him, but he still breathed a sigh of relief when she turned down

Tonya's offer. Scott's girlfriend almost bailed. Courtney was the youngest of the girls at barely sixteen, and she hadn't told her parents she was going out of town. The punishment would be severe if she stayed with Tonya who really didn't want to be left alone even with a crowded bowling alley to wait for her brother. The threat of what her parents might do almost wasn't enough. She was about to cave and stay with Tonya until Michelle begged her not to leave her by herself with three guys.

The girls said goodbye to each other before two of them climbed back in Craig's car to head home. Aaron was the odd man out, and he sat on the other side of Michelle in the front seat. All three girls had been excessively chatty the whole night from the moment they were picked up until the decision to take 116 home was made, but they were suddenly at a loss for words.

Craig wasn't sure if it was the nerves building from driving that stretch of road, or worry over leaving their friend behind. Either way, he was thankful for the silence, but it wouldn't last long. It was exactly twelve miles to Ravenwood, and the guys thought it best to have the car break down at the nine mile mark.

It would make it reasonable to walk to the old castle instead of back to town. Craig would find a reason to venture into the woods shortly after they left the car. They'd hear him scream, followed by silence. No matter how loud they yelled or for how long he wouldn't respond. He'd circle back to the car and inch it down the road with the headlights off, leaving the others to search for him in vain. He'd take his time before returning to the group, giving the girls plenty long enough to jump out of their skin.

He always hated that part of the plan. All of the good stuff would happen while he was gone, and he'd have to settle for the stories. He figured he could hide out in the woods nearby for a bit before heading to the car and maybe catch some of it. There wouldn't be enough light to see anything, but he could at least hear it. By all means, it should be Aaron who disappears since his girlfriend wasn't with them, but this was Craig's car, his baby. No one touched it but him. If they had anticipated Tonya chickening out like she did, they'd have squeezed into Aaron's car instead.

It was too late to think about any of that now. He needed to keep an eye on the road and his mileage. His buddies would be reminded of his sacrifice tonight the next time one of them had to take one for the team.

"How far is it?" asked Courtney from the back seat.

Craig checked the dash. "Not quite four miles," he said. It had been Scott's brilliant last minute idea to reset the trip meter when they turned on 116. He suggested this as a way the girls would know exactly when they could breathe easy again, but really it allowed there to be no arguments over which direction they should walk.

She shivered and sunk back into the seat. "Roll up the window," she said. "I'm cold."

"It's up," he told her.

"Aaron?" she asked. "I feel a draft."

"Mine's up too," Aaron said.

The next five miles passed quickly, but Craig noticed his girlfriend shivered several more times along the way until it was constant. "Are you really that cold?" he asked, blasting the heat.

It felt like an oven almost immediately, and he saw Aaron

instinctively reach for the window crank. Craig eyed him and shook his head. They didn't have long before the car would break down, and he'd give Michelle his jacket. She must be coming down with something. It was warm for April, and she was wearing jeans and a sweater.

Craig glanced at the dash again. *'Shoot.'* They were 9.4 miles out, and he hadn't begun faking car problems yet. He eased his foot off the gas then accelerated hard before leveling off again. The car bucked violently in response.

"Yo, Craig, man," Scott said. "What was that?"

"Not sure," Craig said, shaking his head. "Maybe nothing."

Courtney sat on the edge of the backseat, and Michelle turned around to face her.

'Perfect,' he thought. He manipulated the gas pedal several more times in a row.

The girls were freaking out. They had their heads together over the seat, holding hands, and whispering to each other in high pitched voices that sounded on the verge of tears. Everything was playing out the way they hoped it would aside from Tonya's absence. She'd secretly get a kick out of it when she heard her friends tell her the story tomorrow while being thankful she had stayed behind. When the girls were around, she'd agree with them. The boys had acted horribly and were insufferable, but when she was alone, it'd make her laugh imagining the terror on their faces. She needed to enjoy it while it lasted because they'd get her eventually, and it would be twice as bad.

Craig let off the gas slowly while slamming his hand on the steering wheel and cursing under his breath. The car slowed considerably, and he continued to decrease the speed. They were just past the ten mile mark now, and he had to pull off soon before the opportunity passed.

"Seriously, dude. What's going on?" Aaron asked, leaning across the front seat to peer at the instrument panel.

He didn't respond right away. Aaron's little added touch had almost made him laugh. "Tough to say. Hang on," he said, coming to a stop on the shoulder.

"What are you doing?" Michelle asked. The fear in her voice was so strong it vibrated his soul. "You can't stop here!"

"What choice do I have?" he fired back. "I had the gas to the floor, and we were barely doing twenty." He put the car in park and turned it off then popped the hood. "Stay here," he ordered Michelle. Before opening his door, he turned the key to accessory to use the headlights to see.

He got out and was joined by Aaron and Craig. All three of them stood at the front of the car with the hood propped open, trying hard not to bust out in hysterics. It had been so easy. The girls didn't know the first thing about mechanics and would believe anything they told them. Scott removed a ten cent smoke bomb from his pocket, lit it, and dropped it on the pavement directly in front of the car. White smoke started billowing, and the boys jumped to the side, cursing and waving their arms wildly.

From inside the car, one of the girls screamed. It sounded like Courtney, but it was hard to tell. The boys huddled together and quietly discussed their pleasure in how it was all working out.

Craig went back to the car and opened the door. He sat at the edge of his seat keeping his legs out and broke the news they'd have to walk to Ravenwood. The girls were adamant they weren't leaving the car, and it took longer than anyone anticipated to convince them. By the time all of them started walking, the girls would be in trouble over curfew when they made it home. The fear of their parents hadn't been strong enough to get them moving, but the idea of all three of the guys leaving them in the car to wait alone worked.

According to the trip meter, there was barely more than a mile and half till they reached Ravenwood. Craig waited until they had walked just far enough where it was almost impossible to make out the black Monte Carlo left on the side of the road behind them. "Hold up," he said, trotting across the road.

"Where are you going?" Michelle cried out.

"I gotta take a leak," he yelled back, running into the trees.

It wasn't a lie, but he could've held it if he didn't have an ulterior motive. He leaned against a tree with one hand and took care of business. Their voices carried to him, and he strained an ear to listen after zipping up his jeans. The most he could do was decipher who was talking, but not what was said.

Craig made his way a little farther in the woods, heading straight back. It was dark and dense and would be far too easy to get turned around. He faced the road again, and cupped his hands to his mouth, yelling, "Marco!"

The boys replied, "Polo!"

He made his way back toward the road, and after a few feet, he stopped to make the most dramatic scene he could manage. Small branches were ripped off trees, snapped in two and used to beat the underbrush wildly. Even at this distance, he could hear the girls crying. Their worried voices floated to him, but he couldn't make out their words.

For a couple minutes, he trampled everything he could. He

bent saplings on his crusade, beat trunks of trees with a larger branch that had been laying on the ground, found a few small stones to throw in the direction of his friends, hoping for the best because he couldn't see them in the darkness. Only one bounced along the pavement.

His friends yelled into the woods, "Hey, man! Everything good? What's going on?"

Craig didn't respond right away. He stood there reveling in his accomplishments. It would be a long time before the girls trusted him fully again if they ever did, but it was worth it tonight. Their fear was the one noise he could detect easily.

A scream came from the trees followed by gurgling noises which only lasted seconds then silence. Even the boys seemed concerned which made Michelle and Courtney's terror increase tenfold. Up until now, they held out hope it was a joke, a sick joke at that, but it was still better than the reality. The way the boys reacted, they weren't so sure.

Aaron was the first one to go to the tree line. He went one step at a time, inching closer, yelling out to Craig as he went.

"You okay, dude?"

"This isn't funny."

"Seriously, give it a rest. Did something happen?"

He made it to the edge of the trees and craned his neck from side to side, trying to peer into the woods while calling his friend's name. There was no answer.

The girls hugged each other close and cried softly. Scott kept looking down the road in the direction they came which they thought meant he was considering going back to the car. It was an idea they'd be more than happy to follow. They didn't realize he was checking for Craig's exit from the trees.

"Oh, there you are," Aaron said. "I gotta give you props. You had me shaking in my boots too."

The girls looked at each other. Anger flashed in their eyes, and they exchanged a knowing glance. Craig had done this on purpose. They didn't know without a doubt if the other two were in on it, but of course they had to be. The three boys did everything together. In fact, both girls were wondering if the car was indeed stalled, or if it was a part of the show as well.

There was a loud noise followed by a cut off scream, and when they turned back, Aaron was gone. Scott's complexion had turned sheet white. In the darkness they could see his terror. "Did you see that?" he asked.

The girls shook their heads no. They'd never discuss this night out loud as long as they lived, but if they had, they would discover neither of them knew what to believe anymore at that point. They didn't want to fall for one of their jokes, but if this was a joke, they weren't sure they wanted to see any of these boys ever again.

Scott looked around and clasped both hands on top of his head. He muttered to himself before finally stopping and balling both his hands into fists. "Go back to the car," he said.

Michelle started to protest. "Don't leave us out here."

"You hear me?" he asked angrily. "Go back to the car and wait." He bolted at full speed for the trees. Some long growl coming from his mouth like a suburban war cry.

The wind picked up before he reached the woods. It was a strong wind, blowing them back like special effects straight from a movie set. Scott was knocked down, but fought it to try again. The wind was coming from the woods, and its force kept increasing.

Michelle and Courtney dropped to the road and huddled together. They wrapped their arms and legs around each other to brace themselves from the wild gusts trying to blow them away. They squeezed their eyes shut tight. Both of them crying and yelling, but neither could hear the other over the sound of the gales.

There was another scream followed by another. More and more, the screams of the boys traveled along the gusts, and the volume of their pain and fear increased and decreased as the sound past over the girls. It was all three of them, sounding like their lives were in jeopardy.

Then it stopped. Everything stopped. The winds and the screams disappeared as quickly as it had sprung up. The girls continued to huddle together, afraid of what they would see when they opened their eyes until they heard a whistle followed by the sound of a guy's voice asking if he could be the meat in their sandwich.

Michelle peeked first and gasped. When Courtney opened her eyes and saw what had startled her friend, she almost passed out. They were on the sidewalk on the main drag of Appleton at the corner where Route 116 headed east.

They stood up and started walking. They weren't too familiar with Appleton, least of all this part of the town. There was no real direction behind where they headed, and neither of them spoke. They held hands and leaned into each other, needing to feel the other was still at their side constantly. Down one road then the next, they traveled while taking turns looking over their shoulder for something they wouldn't recognize if it came for them.

After several minutes, they heard it. The sound was faint,

but it was there. They followed it until it became clear then they picked up their pace and headed toward it.

"Marco!" Tonya yelled.

The girls walked past a liquor store, and the bowling alley set back behind the parking lot came into view. "Polo!" they answered.

The three friends reunited as Tonya's brother drove onto the lot. They explained the boys left them when they refused to take Route 116 home with them. Tonya never asked them about what happened that night. In all of her recanting, the girls had never separated. The last time any of them saw the boys was when Craig's car drove off, leaving them stranded at Bowler's Choice Lanes.

Chapter Seven
Change of Plans

Nikolett was a healthy baby girl just as the lady in the woods had foretold. The baby was beautiful with her mom's raven black hair and her father's bright blue eyes. She was everything the young couple had hoped for and more. A year before she was born, they almost lost everything, including each other, and the vow they made would unravel their fate if they broke it.

Keeping true to the word they gave to the lady, Rozalia brought their baby girl to the clearing every day when weather permitted. Some days they'd be there for what could pass as hours, maybe days, with the lady enamored by the child, longing for more time. While on others, they'd be there until dusk searching the trees, and the lady wouldn't even show. It didn't matter. Rozalia would sit in the clearing with her daughter for hours before leaving. If the lady didn't appear right away, she wasn't coming. Still, she wanted to reap the benefits only the clearing, only the sapling could provide. Her child would benefit from the time spent here as well.

Her husband wasn't allowed to enter except by invitation which was rare. The lady expressly forbid it. They weren't sure at first if it was Joseph, or all men, she didn't like, but her tone had suggested it wasn't a topic open to discussion. In time, they gathered the lady's disdain extended to most people, but men faced a fair bit worse from her wrath.

The lady had saved them when they thoughtlessly came to her woods, hoping to start a life together. It was Rozalia's baby, the lady had wanted to save, and she would never be too foolish to forget that. There was no concept of time while the lady fought for them. They had no idea it had taken so long for her to win their freedom from the woods.

Rozalia could make her way to the clearing with her eyes closed in the dark if it weren't for the side of the ravine she had to scale. It wasn't because she memorized the way, muscle memory, or anything of the sort. The clearing called to her. It led a vibrant path straight to it that she could only see in her mind. The invitation had never been extended to Joseph. He had never seen the bright shimmering path.

Instead, he worked hard at making her journey safe, especially now that the baby had arrived. The stairs were built first, even before he cleared a makeshift path from their home to the top of them. While she and Nikolett played in the clearing, he was on the side of the ravine, digging out a narrow walkway for them. Permission to do so, of course, had been given to them by the lady before he touched a single fallen leaf. While they believed no harm would befall Rozalia as mother to the child the lady adored, they also understood Joseph was lucky to be alive.

The clearing was just ahead, and as she approached it, a shadow moved on the far side. The lady was here already, waiting on them. This was unexpected. Rozalia wondered what news she brought that she couldn't wait to come until after they had arrived. She shivered at the thought. It couldn't be good.

Rozalia stepped inside the clearing and heard the twisting and cracking sounds of the branches as they grabbed hold of each other tightly, forming an impenetrable bond. It confirmed the lady was present. They only encapsulated the area to protect the lady they served. That was something else she and Joseph had learned while they waited on the lady to allow them to return home. Once inside, not only did time essentially come to a halt, but it was up to the trees, and the lady who ruled them, if you were allowed to leave.

The lady approached her and took Nikolett from her arms, dancing her around the sapling and singing something that sounded both familiar and foreign to Rozalia. It tugged on her memory as if she should recognize it even though she was certain this was the first time she'd heard it. The only thing for her to do now was wait.

There were many types of trees in the circle around the clearing. Rozalia wasn't familiar with most of them. Even the ones she recognized she couldn't name. She couldn't tell an oak from a maple. Joseph taught her the differences in the leaves many times, but the knowledge never stuck. She'd forget again and have them confused by the next time she wondered about it. Looking around the edge of the circle, she was curious about them. Some of the trees she hadn't seen anywhere else in the woods except this clearing. The variety added to both the allure and mystique of this location.

It was hard to track the passage of time once the trees closed around them. The light of the day was completely blocked, but the clearing remained well lit. To Rozalia, it may feel like a couple hours, but the sun will be rising on tomorrow when she leaves. Any attempts to track it had failed. Watches stopped working in the clearing with or without interference from the trees. It was the sapling's doing, but the sapling's secrets were heavily guarded along with the lady's.

Rozalia settled in for a long wait. It had been nearly two weeks since the lady had appeared, and she expected her husband to suffer days without either of them before she left in no less than several hours to head home. To her amazement, she returned to her side with Nikolett after only one song. It must be a big storm brewing if she was limiting her time with the baby.

He hadn't checked his watch, but it couldn't have been more than five minutes after his wife's departure before he saw her walking toward him again. His heart skipped a beat with worry. This didn't bode well. Their agreement was Rozalia didn't have to wait. If the lady didn't appear when she arrived, she was free to go, having fulfilled her end of the promise, but his wife always basked in the glow of the sapling for as long as she could stand the solitude.

Joseph smiled warmly at her. "Everything alright?" he asked. He could see through the smile she gave him in return.

"This is enough for today," she said, nodding toward the shovel in his hand. "Let's go. There's been a change of plans."

On their long walk back to their home, Rozalia filled him in on the new plans for the castle. They would immediately set to work on transforming it into an inn. The sooner it was open for business, the happier the woods surrounding them would be.

Expansion was exploding all around them. The nearest communities had been over a day away then new towns closed in on them by hours. Small communities were growing into small cities not far from the woods they vowed to protect. Something needed to be done to keep people at bay, but the woods weren't strong enough to do it on their own.

That's where the Weavers came in to the plan. They would draw people to this part of the countryside, luring them with the appeal of exploring an authentic castle, staying the night reminiscent of how European royalty lived their everyday life. Perhaps they could host weddings with the castle serving as an elegant backdrop to young couples saying their vows as they began their life together. Whatever they did, it had to work. Visitors needed to come to Ravenwood.

"They want people?" Joseph's shock was deep. "I thought they wanted to be left alone?"

Rozalia shook her head as they walked through a door in the back of their home, leading to the kitchen. She set Nikolett in her wooden high chair, tucking a small blanket around her sides and back to keep her from slouching over since she wasn't sitting on her own yet. There was enough light coming through to see by, but barely. Not wanting the constant hum of the electric lights which grated her head until it ached, she lit a couple oil lamps. The day was still early, and she wasn't used to being in the kitchen before the light from the sun made its way across the sky to the back of Ravenwood.

Dinner was in the icebox for Joseph to put on when he finished his work in the ravine where she left it every morning before heading to the clearing. She looked around the kitchen, wondering how to spend the day since it was rare for her to have one to herself during the warm summer weather. No, there was plenty to do. The castle needed to be adapted for guests.

Ideas ticked off in her mind. There were enough rooms to run a small inn, but bathrooms weren't in large supply. They could offer shared bathrooms like the hostels in Europe, but it wasn't a guarantee the people of this country, with their spoiled upbringings, would settle for such a concept. As she paced the floor sorting through any options coming to her, she noticed her husband staring at her, waiting for something. "What?" she asked him.

"Did you not hear me?" he asked, coming near.

Rozalia searched for what he may have said, but for the life of her, she couldn't remember her husband speaking. "No, sorry. I have a lot on my mind."

"Why the change of heart?" Why do the woods want visitors all of a sudden?" he asked.

She opened her mouth, but stopped short of speaking. The words were there. They would be easy to repeat. It sounded so simple and logical when the lady put the message in her head as she handed Nikolett back less than an hour ago. Repeating the words out loud was harder than she expected. Her heart beat faster, and she put her hand to her chest without thinking.

"What is it?" he asked, reaching out to touch her arm. His wife wasn't able to hide anything from him, and he could see something was deeply upsetting her.

"They're hungry," she said softly.

Joseph stepped away from his wife, recoiling from her words. Both of them had a general idea of what went on in the woods. They'd almost been victims of the trees themselves, but neither of them talked about it. If they ignored it and acted like going to a clearing every day was a normal occurrence for most people, it made them feel better, like they had nothing to do with it. That was because they didn't have anything to do with it, and there wasn't much they could do about it short of burning it all to the ground.

It was something he'd considered many times. He used to stay awake at night wondering how he could unburden himself and his family of this situation. There was no easy way out. If he managed to destroy it all, they'd have nowhere to go. That was if he even survived, if they survived. Whatever ruled the trees would make it through the fire. He'd bet on it. The force that was out there, surrounding them, watching them, controlling them, would find them again if they made it out alive.

"Hungry?" he asked quietly. The word came out of his mouth more to break the silence than because he needed an answer. There was only one thing it could mean. The lady wanted them to bring unsuspecting guests to the woods for dinner, only the visitors would be the main course.

"They're weak," Rozalia said. "With everything springing up nearby, there's going to be more trespassers, a lot more."

There hadn't been much proof of it so far. From time to time, someone would go missing. The police would come around asking questions. The person had been traveling through the area or had been known to venture off in the woods and maybe went a little farther this time, stumbling onto the Weaver property by accident.

The truth was they had no information to give the police, but deep down, they assumed whoever it was met their fate in the woods surrounding their home. The stories associated with this land had been circulating since the colonists, his ancestors, first made their way this far west. Joseph never thought of them as more than stories until he brought his new wife out here to see where they would live.

"They want us to bring more people here," he nodded. This was why they were changing from their solitude. The trees needed their strength. "Wouldn't the trespassers be enough? They'd get stronger each time."

Rozalia shook her head, and her eyes glistened. The tears she wanted to unleash would have to stay contained unless she risk offending the trees. They could sense her inside her home as easily as they could when she walked among them. "The strength they gain is temporary. If a group of hikers came through a couple months after their last meal," she said heavily, "they wouldn't be able to defend themselves."

Joseph sat at the table and watched Nikolett. She was such a happy baby and found amusement in hitting the tray of her high chair. It rattled against the arms, and the noise made her laugh. He worried about her future, what would happen when she came of age, and if the trees would allow her to leave. The burden belonged to him and his wife, but the lady's attachment to Nikolett concerned him. They were helpless to do anything.

They had tried once shortly after Nikolett's birth. The three of them went to Boston to visit his family although it was merely a ruse. His family deserved to meet his daughter no more than the strangers they passed on the trip. The plans, however, had been very real. He alone held the truth, and he pushed it from his mind until they were settled for the night in a hotel not far from where his parents moved after they learned their son had survived the woods.

His parents were callous and cared only about appearances. When he married Rozalia after she nursed him back to health during the war, he expected them to resist her. He didn't expect the lack of concern they'd show her family when all believed them to be dead. What's worse is the talk surrounding their reappearance forced them into hiding, giving them no choice but to move to the coast.

Because he was afraid the trees were capable of detecting his lie even if it was never spoken out loud, they did visit his parents. Briefly. They went to his parents' home with the intention of showing off Nikolett from the stoop, never entering the house. The man who answered the door was no one Joseph recognized, but he slammed the door in their faces at the mention of their names. It was all the same to Joseph. He hadn't made a liar of himself.

The lady had been advised of the trip and how long it would take. Rozalia assured her they'd spend one night in Boston. They'd arrive around noon, spend time with the Weaver's, and then leave the next day. It's what she told the lady because it's the plans Joseph had conveyed to her. He couldn't involve his wife in his treachery in case it was found out.

When he suggested a longer visit, Rozalia objected as he suspected she might. He convinced her another night wouldn't be a problem. They'd explain to the lady afterward they wanted to tour the city. After all, it wasn't like the roots of the trees could reach them over a hundred miles away.

There was never a time in his life when he had been more wrong. When he woke the next morning, he was feeling ill. They feared it was a remnant he had contracted of the Spanish Flu and called a doctor right away, but he had never seen anything like it. The illness Joseph had consumed him within hours, and he presumed he was on his death bed. His reigning consolation was the trees wouldn't gain anything from his departure. They were too far from Ravenwood for the woods to harness his dark energy.

It was Rozalia who understood better than he did. She believed it was the lady of the woods who was bringing about his demise for lying to her. In all they're years together, Joseph never told her the truth about his plans for Boston, but she had her suspicions. Even if it was an impromptu decision to extend their stay, the lady was unhappy.

No one understood her reasoning for leaving when her husband was in such a weakened state. They needn't have to comprehend or even agree with her decision; they needed only to help her load him once he was unconscious. The doctor had explained as delicately as possible there was nothing he could do. Whatever ailment had overtaken her husband was going to bring about his end. The only thing she could do was be by his side and pray.

Rozalia convinced everyone at the hotel she wanted to try to bring him to his home before he passed to give everyone a chance to say goodbye. They assumed there was family waiting on them at Ravenwood which is what she wanted them to believe. As each mile passed on their way home, her husband's condition miraculously improved. By the time they reached the manor, he was in tip top shape, showing zero signs of having almost succumbed to the hold the woods held over them.

The woods had come for him, and he never tried anything so drastic again as he didn't know how far they could reach. He considered Boston a warning. If he was foolish enough to risk a second attempt, the lady's anger would be swift, and he feared, far more painful. His wife saved his life and not for the first time.

Looking at Nikolett, he hoped their burden would end with the two of them. He prayed the woods wouldn't continue their control over his daughter too.

"What do we need to do?" he asked, hanging his head in defeat.

Rozalia reached across the table and patted his hand. "We convert the manor into an inn. It will take a lot of work, but they'll help us as they always have. All we have to do is bring people to the grounds. The woods will do the rest."

Chapter Eight
Sisters

Jules couldn't remember much of anything before the age of five. It had been extremely hot the day she wandered onto the newly constructed path around Ravenwood Manor. Back then, the path wasn't much more than a dirt trail through the woods. It was declared the only safe passage through the trees by the owners of the property. A cheap barrier guided guests in the form of a rope strung through metal posts sticking out of the ground every few feet.

No one was on the path that day. No one dared venture outside with the temperature reaching over a hundred degrees, a rare feat in western Massachusetts.

Someone had told her to follow the path. She was sure of it, but she could never remember who it was that told her. It was assumed by many she found the path on her own and followed it naturally. That was an explanation she could never buy. On that day, the first day of her life, she didn't know what a path was, or a sidewalk or a road. None of that had existed before she showed up in the manor's courtyard, not wearing a stitch of clothing.

There had been nobody outside, and she was admiring the fountain in the gardens when one of the guests saw her through their window. Word of the naked child with light brown sun kissed hair who was playing outside spread quickly through Ravenwood, and everyone rushed out to cover her, to help her, to see who she belonged to, but no one recognized her. The child appeared to be in good health, well taken care of, and clean aside from the bottom of her feet which were covered in dirt.

Even the Weavers looked surprised to find the little girl on their property. The secrets they keep, keep secrets of their own.

The commotion scared her. Everyone was talking to her at once. It was a language she was familiar with, but had rarely spoke. The bulk of the words she recognized, but the meanings were lost. Most of their questions didn't make sense, like who were her parents.

'What were parents?'

A woman wrapped her in a robe which she fought. Her skin was already burning since coming out from under the shade of the trees. The robe added to her discomfort, but the woman insisted.

It was the reason why she took to religion so easily when the family who brought her into their home introduced her to it. The story of Eve and the apple fascinated her. Like Eve, she didn't know she was naked until somebody pointed it out.

Everyone was making such a fuss over her. She tried to pull away, tried to make it back to the woods where she felt safe. A man scooped her up and carried her inside the castle while her little fists pelted his back with weak punches.

He brought her to a room with several tables and chairs. Everyone else was kept out except for one woman, his wife. She was the woman who insisted on wrapping her in the heavy robe. They continued to pepper her with questions she didn't understand and talked about things she had never before heard.

'What's a phone call?'

The woman placed something she had never seen in front of her on the table. It was see through and contained an orange liquid. Jules didn't know what to do with it until she watched the man lift a similar white object to his mouth and take a drink.

Jules followed his example and lifted the glass to her lips, taking a sip. It was sweet, but tart. It had an overall pleasing taste, but it made her mouth cry out in what was almost a painful reaction.

To this day, she won't drink orange juice.

The woman asked, "You don't like it?"

That's when Jules spoke the one and only word she uttered while at Ravenwood. "Water."

The woman smiled and nodded at her. She took the glass away and returned with another clear glass filled with the only drink she could identify.

A man dressed in a dark outfit and boots, which looked too hot for the temperature outside, arrived at the manor first. A kind, older woman joined him not long afterward. One of them gave her a shirt. It was white with a pocket on the front. She couldn't remember who gave it to her or even putting it on, but it hung off her like an oversized dress when the two of them walked her outside, helping her into the woman's car.

The woman put her in the front seat. Maybe it was to be nice. Maybe it was because the backseat was mostly covered with a box and various papers strewn across it. Before they pulled out of the parking lot, the woman offered her a piece of gum with a smile so bright, Jules couldn't say no.

She didn't know she wasn't supposed to swallow it.

When they got to the hospital, the man in the dark outfit was there. Everyone else wore white. Their clothes matched the color of the shirt she had been given.

Jules never wears white.

The next several weeks were a literal nightmare. The stress and fear they provoked were worse than anything else she ever faced in life. Even now at the age of fifty, she still jumps awake in the middle of the night in a cold sweat, having dreamt about those days.

It was all questions, police, and doctors. They asked for her name and her parents' name so many times. She learned to tell by the look on their face it was the question they were about to ask next.

'What's a name?'

They tried to examine her, but she fought them at every turn. They stabbed at her with small, thin, sharp objects and shone blinding lights into her eyes. They had her lay this way and that way while looking at every inch of her body. She fought them off until she couldn't anymore. Looking back, she knows they gave her a sedative, but at the time, she had no understanding of what that could be. All the frightened child version of herself knew was she wanted to fight, but she couldn't. Her body wouldn't do what her mind was asking it to any longer. That was scarier yet.

There were words and phrases she heard many times over the next couple weeks while at the hospital, the police station, and what they called a foster home. *Missing children*, but she was only one child. No signs of *sexual or physical abuse*. Both were phrases she asked about, hoping someone would explain them to her, but no one ever did. They determined she had *amnesia* which must have been brought on by *psychological trauma* since there were no signs of a physical injury which could've caused it.

She overheard her foster mother whom she called Maggie talking to the kind old woman who gave her that first piece of gum. The older woman said news of her discovery had made it as far as Mississippi.

"What's the Mississippi?" she had asked.

They looked at her surprised, probably because it was so rare for her to speak. Maggie said, "It's a very large river in the middle of the United States. You'll learn about it in school."

'What's a school?'

'What's the United States?'

Jules learned quickly not to ask questions because the answers only led to more questions.

The man in the dark outfit came to visit her many times, and he'd bring his wife when he did. They'd take her to the park, the zoo, and they'd always take her out to eat. When her family couldn't be located and nobody stepped forward to claim her, they asked if she would like to live with them, for them to be her mom and dad.

Her understanding of the words mom and dad was rough at best. The other children in the home where she lived all had a different opinion of those words. Some hated their moms and dads and wanted nothing to do with them. Others longed for the day when they might find a mom and dad of their own.

Jules knew she was supposed to go with the man, but just like her decision to walk along the path, she couldn't remember how she knew this was what she should do. It was like she had a memory of someone telling her Officer Dixon will take care of you, but she couldn't remember who said it to her or even hearing the words.

The officer and his wife couldn't have children, but they always wanted a family. The Saturday she stumbled upon the courtyard of Ravenwood manor was the day after the doctor's appointment where they learned his wife was barren. The first call of his shift that day had been about a young girl who had been found wandering out of the woods alone.

He knew the moment he received the call this young girl was meant to find him. Later that night when he told his wife, she believed it as well. This wasn't a coincidence. Jules was their miracle. Julia Marie was the name Ruth Dixon had chosen for her daughter years before she even met her husband.

A birth certificate was created for her. Without any information from Jules to go on, they gave her the birthday of August 2nd, the day she was found. Doctors guessed her age to be around five years old. August 2, 1970, was the birth date she'd always celebrated, but she often wondered when her real birthday actually was.

The modern world is an amazing time to be alive. Advancements in computers, science and medicine all led her to this moment. As soon as she heard of a DNA test which could track her ancestry, she sent away for it. The cost was not a concern. It wasn't because she didn't love her parents. She did. She wouldn't trade them for anyone in the world, including her biological ones.

Jules knew taking this test was opening a Pandora's Box, but she also knew she could refuse contact if she wanted to. She didn't want to know her biological parents. She was curious, but unsure about if she had any blood siblings. Her parents adopted two more children after her, and they along with her own children, nieces, and nephews were all the family she needed. This DNA test held the potential of providing the answer to the one question she had never been able to learn.

'When is my real birthday?'

It took over ten years. A decade of waiting and wondering passed before she finally got a hit. The hope and excitement springing forth from it consumed her every waking thought and was quickly dashed. It was followed by disappointment in what she assumed had been not just one, but two faulty tests.

Susan Horn had never married and never had children only because she was from an era when you did not have children out of wedlock. The reason she swore off marriage is because of what happened to her own mother.

Sandy, her baby sister, started crying in response to the fighting. Susan wanted to cry too, but the sound would have helped her father find her. Something broke. It was a plate, but Susan didn't know that when she heard the crash. That's what started the fight. Her father began yelling and using words which would earn her a mouth full of soap if she ever repeated them.

Susan opened the dormer window of her bedroom and carefully slid out onto the roof. She crawled up the side and sat on top of it. This was the only hiding spot her father hadn't found yet.

She had worked up the nerve a few months ago to run away. She loaded a paper sack with an outfit, a toothbrush, her teddy bear, a peanut butter and jelly sandwich, and all of the money she had in her piggy bank, totaling sixty-seven cents. Then she waited for her father to pass out. It was taking too long, and she was getting tired.

That's when she decided to climb out on the roof and jump to the ground. Once outside her window, the street light was bright enough to show her the ground was farther away then she originally thought. She went back in her room and lost her nerve to run away after that, but it hadn't been a total loss. The hiding spot came in handy far too often.

It was because she was on the roof she didn't hear anything else taking place in the house. She didn't hear the thud every time her dad's fist made contact with her mom, although it was a sound she knew well. She didn't hear her dad cry out once he'd realized what he had done, that he'd taken it too far this time. She did hear him call her name when he came into her room as he searched for her. Susan closed her eyes and prayed instead of answering him.

When he left her room, she didn't move. She didn't hear him as he ran through the house, throwing things in suitcases, and packing everything in the car. She did hear him fire up the Bel Air and pull out of the driveway, thankful her bedroom was on the back of the house where he wouldn't see her on the roof.

That's when she came inside, surprised the baby had stopped crying, and her mama had managed to calm Sandy down so soon. Susan softly made her way out of her room and down the stairs. The house was eerily silent. Her mama usually cried for hours after a fight like this.

She walked down the hall to the kitchen and saw the pieces of the plate on the floor next to her mama's legs. She didn't go any further, but turned and ran to the neighbor's house. Even though she didn't see anything above her mama's knees, she knew her mama was dead.

Her father and baby sister were never seen again. The Bel Air was found some twenty-two years later in a ravine less than an hour north of where she had been born. A couple had been walking a trail with a pair of binoculars, doing some bird watching, when they spied it. No one could really explain how the car had made it so far off the highway. The best theory was the road blocks set up shortly after the neighbors called the police that night might have caused her father to go off road which led to the crash. The investigation was closed as a car accident resulting in the death of both of them even when the only body, or what was left of it, recovered was her father's. Susan tuned out when the talk turned to remains, scavenger animals and rate of decomposition to explain why nothing of her sister's body was found.

For twenty-two years, she believed they were alive somewhere, and she might one day be reunited with her baby sister. That dream was shattered by a couple hoping to spot a scissor-tailed flycatcher.

The only reason she even submitted the DNA test was at her nieces and nephews' insistence. Her adopted brother had a house full of children, more than enough to make up for Susan never having any. They had bought kits for themselves as well because they wanted to know more about her and their father's biological families. It was never her desire to reconnect. Any family who could produce a monster the likes of her father was a family better left alone in her opinion. She loved her nieces and nephews like they were her own, and for them, she'd do anything.

The results of the original test showed her sister was still alive, but after emailing her, the dream was shattered again. There had been a mistake. Both women decided to resubmit the tests, figuring there must be a blood correlation between the two. It just couldn't be one as direct as the results suggested. When the second set of tests produced the same results, it was heartbreaking, and Susan lost her faith in the science behind them.

If Susan had given Jules a chance and taken the time to get to know her, she would've learned about the strange origins of Jules' childhood. She had emerged from the path into the gardens at Ravenwood no more than a mile from where the Bel Air was later spotted. Maybe they would've thought it more than mere coincidence, but Susan never extended that hospitality.

Jules looked through the few pictures Susan Horn had emailed her when they first matched. It didn't add up. The picture of Susan standing near the cake on her sixteenth birthday looked identical enough to her at the same age to be her twin. They might be related, but it was impossible they were sisters like the genealogy website proclaimed.

She opened the last email Susan had sent her, insisting the second test results had also been a mistake. There must have been a mix up at the lab, some contamination of the DNA swabs. Jules stared at what Susan wrote about her sister Sandy.

Not for the first time in her life, it was a language she understood. The bulk of the words she recognized. However, the meaning behind them was lost.

Her husband walked up behind her and placed his hand on her shoulder. "What are you thinking? Do you want to retest?"

Jules shook her head no and logged out of her email before shutting down the computer.

"Are you going to meet her?" he asked. "There's five years of your life you don't remember. Maybe there's something she could tell you that would jog a memory."

Jules looked at him and smiled. "No. The only thing I wanted was to learn when my real birthday was," she said, thinking about the words in Susan's email. "I know it now. It's August 2, 1970."

The doctors had to guess her approximate age, and a birthday had been created for her. Being born on March 30, whether it was four months earlier or eight months later than their guess was one thing, but it would have been impossible for them to get the year so wrong. There was no way she was born in 1955.

Chapter Nine
Scare Tactics

Bobby worried about his sister and regretted ever bringing her to Ravenwood to apply for the front desk position. It had been their parents' idea, but he wished he had told them there were no openings. He didn't work the front desk, so he wouldn't have extra shifts giving away the lie. Once he mentioned Ravenwood was hiring, he couldn't take it back. Even so, he could've only pretended to take Alice there to apply and later, to interview.

It had crossed his mind to pretend, but he considered himself a decent guy. He didn't lie to his parents as a rule. Given the situation with his sister and how tight money was at home, they'd be pretty irate to hear he helped Alice pass on a job opportunity if they found out. He could keep it to himself, but Alice was another story. She'd always felt like she played second fiddle to him. Mom definitely had a soft spot for her son, but their dad babied his sister. The mistreatment was from how he felt about women having a place in society. That place was at home, running the house and family. Alice wanted more than that, and she grew to resent not having her dad in her corner.

Bobby had done what he could to help Alice bomb the interview, to guarantee she'd never be offered a job. All she had to do was remain calm and clear headed throughout it.

Ravenwood fed on fear. Alice had been so angry he hadn't explained it to her completely, but it would've made things worse. He couldn't tell her there were ghosts, spirits, something at Ravenwood, and whatever it was could sense how she felt, feed off it, and grow stronger. She'd probably have a breakdown from stepping onto the grounds if he had.

There was probably some happy medium, some solution he could've tried to prevent this, but it was too late to worry about that now. What's done was done. Alice needed to settle in at the manor because she was giving the woods too much power.

All new employees went through this to a lesser degree. It was unnerving to work there, and only the ones with the most energy to offer the woods were hired. Things would settle after a while. It varied for everyone, but two to three months seemed to be about average. Whenever a new employee was hired, the seasoned staff prepared for a massive influx in activity. Every startle, every scream, every increased heartbeat caused by the strange goings on added more fuel to the fire. New hires were considered fresh blood. No one ever became too complacent in the things that happened inexplicably, but the shock value did begin to wane. As it did, everyone settled into their old routines, but for the introductory period, they'd all have their guard up.

It had been six months, and if anything, Alice's fear had only grown stronger. Everyone else grew used to items being moved around or unexplained noises, and they learned to laugh at it instead of being frightened. Not his sister. If anything, Alice was more apprehensive over it. Her fear fed the manor, or the lady of the woods, maybe they are one and the same, but whatever was feeding off her, it was gaining power.

Every time something scared her, Ravenwood's power surged which meant more activity thrown at the staff, including his sister which triggered the loop all over again. It was a vicious cycle resulting in the continuous increase of some not easily explained supernatural being. There are those who could explain it, could shed much desired light on the forces that reckoned, but they choose not to, trying to act as though the tales told for decades were no more than overactive imaginations. The Weaver family excelled at keeping secrets.

Still, the problem of Alice's reactions remained. The owners regaled her as their prized asset, and of course, they would see it that way. If fear could be harnessed as energy for the living, his sister would provide electricity for the entire state. The Weavers had what they wanted. Their demons, personal or otherwise, were satiated, but it was at the risk of his sister's sanity.

The rest of the staff were growing listless with it as well. Yes, they'd been acclimated to working here and knew what to expect with new hires, but everything usually died down quicker than this. Instead of small objects like pens being moved around, all the tables in a room would stack on top of each other in a pile in the time it took someone to pick up something off the floor. Items were going missing from housekeeping carts only to be found on the trails, or in the break rooms, or some other absurd location.

Things probably wouldn't have become so heated if nothing had happened to Penny. She was one of the newer housekeeping staff, and everyone enjoyed working with her. The cart she had pulled flush against the doorway of a room she was cleaning disappeared. When she stepped into the hall to see where it was, it came flying at full speed in her direction. She ran from it down the hall instead of running back into the room and into the elevator. The cart followed her inside, pinning her against the back of it before the doors closed.

The elevator got stuck between floors, and the fired department had to be called out. By the time they pried the doors open, she was sitting on the floor of the elevator next to the cart, hugging her knees to her chest. Thankfully, there were no injuries. She didn't quit either, but something changed in her. The usually upbeat and bright disposition was gone, and she barely spoke to anyone after that. Everyone could feel the shift occurring in the manor. It was making everyone feel on edge, and there had been rumors.

They'd never fire Alice. She could call in four days in a row, no show for a week, and the owners would welcome her back. All of the employees were aware of this too. They wanted to make her quit, but they also had at least a general idea of why she couldn't.

Their parents would flip out if she did, so she had no choice but to stick it out here until she found another job. It wasn't for lack of trying. She'd been saving every penny she could to buy a car and get far away from Route 116 and Ravenwood. Dad got laid off a couple weeks after she started here, and she had been giving her money to help the household out. There wasn't much going into her savings anymore. Bobby had been trying everything he could to help his sister in the meantime, but nothing had worked.

Bobby attempted everything short of slipping something into her drink to take the edge off for his sister. The more he told her to relax, think of it as harmless pranks from co-workers, or to let go and laugh at it like the rest of them, the worse she became. He laid it all out to her, explaining it will all die down once her nerves do.

The staff wasn't being forthcoming with him about their plan, but he heard whispers of how they were going to try to scare her so badly she'd run out and never return. He hoped to solve the problem before they had a chance, but he couldn't. Everything about it, from bringing his sister to the interview in the first place to being unable to put her at ease, soon became his biggest life regret.

It was late into a Monday shift during the winter when the manor's business was on the slow side. They didn't cut anyone's hours, but sometimes added to their duties to pad out the shift. Alice was given some housekeeping duties in the offices behind the front desk, including the break room and employee bathroom. She didn't mind the work, but hated how it took her out of the public area of the lobby where she felt safer because she wasn't always alone. That time of night in the back, there was almost never anyone else around.

That's why some of the employees picked then to strike. It was also Bobby's day off which meant he wouldn't be around to protect her. Three of them were going to wait until after she took her last break and hide. They'd each scare her as she made her way through the areas off limits to guests, ticking off her to-do list. Everyone else would cover for them, but they could still get in trouble if they were found out, specifically if Alice ratted them out for it. It was a risk they were willing to take if it meant getting rid of her for good.

Becky hid under Mrs. Weaver's desk, waiting for Alice to come along and empty the small waste bin. She was going to jump out and startle her when the time was right. Viv went to the bathroom. It had been remodeled in the fifties to include a full shower and bath tub. If any employees found themselves stranded, they could sleep on a cot in the office instead of dirtying up one of the manor's guest rooms. She stood in the tub and pulled the curtain close, waiting for her opportunity. Jerry waited until Alice left the break room then ducked inside. He stood behind the door until she came back to clean it. They figured the three scares should be enough to do the trick, but if not, her fear tonight would make the manor more overactive than it'd ever been. It seemed foolproof she'd run out without looking back before her shift ended.

Becky heard the door when Alice came into the room to begin cleaning. The other two wouldn't get a head's up until she opened the doors to the rooms they were in as well, but they might be lucky enough to hear Alice scream. Becky wasn't sure if she'd be able to hang around to witness the whole show without alerting Alice that something else might be staged for her.

When Alice came around the back of the desk and grabbed the small waste bin, nothing happened. Becky never made her move. Alice didn't like to be in the office alone. She didn't like to be anywhere in the manor alone, but the office always made her feel like she was doing something wrong, like she wasn't supposed to be there without one of the owners present. She grabbed the bin and dumped it in the larger bag attached to a housecleaning cart and moved on with the rest of the work on her list. If she had looked closer, if she had moved the desk chair, she might have seen Becky's feet half sliding, half kicking along the carpet as the cord for the telephone that ran under the desk cut into her throat, blocking her ability to breathe.

If she had made it to the break room, she would've been the one to find Jerry, but a late check in brought her back to the front desk. It was one of the housekeepers, thinking the pranks played on Alice were long over, who swung the door wide enough to knock Jerry into the wall. The woman screamed. It echoed throughout the entire downstairs of the manor. Luckily, the new guests had gone up to their room only minutes before the shrillness of her voice pierced the lobby.

Alice could feel her fear. The woman's scream echoed through the small hall into the office and burst through the open door behind the reception area with enough force to knock Alice forward into the desk. Her hands gripped the edge of the counter until her knuckles turned white. Everything happened in slow motion, and her ears didn't register the subsequent shouts as more than a dull echo. Her heart pounded hard enough to almost hurt, and she worried if it would hold out. The sound of each beat vibrated through her body and rattled her ear drums. Behind her, she could hear a woman's voice, crying now, sobbing, but still calling out for help. It sounded so distant like she was on the other side of the woods on the property line instead of maybe thirty feet away.

There was no way for her to know what caused the alarm, but she *knew*. It was Ravenwood. Someone had fallen victim to whatever curse haunted this property. Alice had to go back there, to see if she could help although she rightfully assumed she could not, but her feet wouldn't move, and her eyes wouldn't break their gaze away from the small, round silver service bell on top of the counter where they fixated as she focused on breathing. *'Breathe in.'*

The words went through her head as she sucked a gulp of air into her lungs. *'Breathe out.'*

The air tickled her lips as it slowly flowed out of her mouth. Nothing in her body operated automatically anymore. Alice even told her heart when to beat.

She told herself to turn, to help, to see if there was anything she could do, at least act the way a person would behave in normal circumstances. The housekeeper was sitting against the wall in the hallway with her knees to her chest. Her face was buried into her legs, but her whole body shook, giving away her sobs which barely registered to Alice's ears.

The doorway to the break room was slightly ajar, and through the small crack between the door and the frame she could see a body lying on the floor. All she could see was a pair of legs inside the dark blue maintenance uniform. It was Jerry. He was the only one on this shift who was wearing that color.

Frozen in the hallway, she stared at his legs. They weren't moving, not even the smallest twitch. The name of the woman sitting in hysterics wasn't registering to her even though she knew her well enough. In fact, she barely took notice of her except for the dull echo of her cries that seemed to be coming from far away, not five feet to her left.

Alice was numb. Her heart still thudded loudly in her chest, but it was decreasing, both in rhythm and intensity. The way she breathed was controlled and automatic without having to remind herself of each breath she took. She had a curiosity and an understanding. The woods took Jerry, but how and why were still a mystery added to the already long list of ones that would never be solved.

There was a commotion, and she turned her head without

removing her gaze. Someone else was coming, running down the hall to see what happened. He knelt before the poor woman and shouted at Alice. The sound hit her ears, but the words did not. She stepped back just in time for him to enter the break room.

She turned and walked to her station at the reception desk. Life was still moving in slow motion. Walking felt like she was under water. It was slow and deliberate, much slower than she believed herself to be moving. Everything sounded distant, and the lights even glowed brighter than usual. As soon as she stepped out of the back rooms to the small work area behind the counter, life caught up. As if on fast forward, she felt a push that slammed into her while the reality around her increased its speed. The room spun for a moment, and she placed a hand on the wall to steady her. Then the sounds rushed in, loud and clear for the first time.

The Weavers were the first call she made after closing the door to the back rooms. They were in their room and made it to the lobby before anyone answered the police line she called. Alice stayed at the desk, following orders, and manning the phones, trying to avoid the scene unfolding behind her. As people came and went through the office door, she picked up enough here and there to figure out what happened.

The door hit him hard enough to break his nose, but that was the least of his injuries. There was a glass case on the wall used to cover a bulletin board peppered with state mandated literature as well as employee news. His head hit it perfectly.

It almost looked like he was trying to come out from behind the door, whether to protect his face or because something else moved him, would always be a source of gossip for the manor and area towns. The glass shattered and shards pierced his skull. The metal edge of the case sliced into him as well. The authorities would question how he had struck the case with enough force just from being hit by the break room door, but would ultimately chalk it up to an accidental death.

Bobby learned later there was more than met the eye that night, but he wasn't sure if his sister knew the whole truth. He would certainly never tell her. The late night check in was lost in the country side, battling the storm, hoping to find a town before they ran out of gas. A young woman with flowing raven hair was freezing on the side of the road with her thumb out in hopes of finding a ride to Ravenwood. The couple had never heard of the manor before and thought themselves incredibly lucky to be so close to shelter.

The other two were never seen again after that night. The owners insisted they must have quit on the spot with Jerry's tragic death occurring so soon after Penny's accident. There was talk in the area. From time to time, someone would claim to have seen either Becky or Viv. They were spotted everywhere from Hartford to Boston. Their families reported them missing, but the police did little for two adults who seemingly ran off together, especially after learning the last place they were seen was Ravenwood. An officer never came to the manor to talk to anyone about them.

It changed his sister. At work, she was calm. When faced with a surge in activity around the grounds, Alice was unaffected. Bobby couldn't get her to say much about it except she appreciated them now. *'Appreciated? Ravenwood?'* He shook his head and never asked again. The differences in Alice didn't end when she clocked out and went home. For the rest of her life, she was neutral, numb, a zombie version of her former spark going through the motions. She either refused to show emotion, or was incapable of it.

The housekeeper who entered the break room that night was never the same. She came back to work to the utter shock of everyone, including the owners. It took over a month of inpatient therapy before she drove onto the grounds again. From that night forward, she did her job and went home. The only co-worker she talked to after that was Alice. The rest of the staff believed something was in that break room, and she saw it. That's why she came back. She was afraid of being its next victim. That's why she befriended Alice because she understood now, better than anyone else, the fear that controlled her.

Chapter Ten
No One to Hear You Cry

It was supposed to be a short hike. Jeff had pulled into the little parking area off Dunberry Road just after eleven that morning. They were pleased to see only two other cars in the lot and no one in the playground and picnic area near the start of the trail.

Winter was refusing to cede its grip to spring this year. The high was only supposed to reach the mid-sixties, and the rain over the last week would've left the trail mostly muddy. They didn't expect to see a lot of people out, but the Shaw Memorial Park was widely popular in this half of the state.

Daniel Shaw had been a well-respected county officer. The entrance to the park marked the location where he was killed. He was struck down during a routine traffic stop by a drunk driver, leaving behind a wife and five children under the age of nine.

That wasn't the park's only draw. The far side of the trail was five miles from Ravenwood property. The park was popular because people could get the thrill of being on the edge of danger. Some spun a few yarns themselves about venturing off the trail and tempting fate by wandering so close to it without the risk of actually stepping foot inside its borders.

They sat at one of the tables and had what Jeff called a lazy man's picnic: a sub sandwich they picked up on the drive. They chatted for a while after their meal to let their food settle before they attempted the hike.

Ashley had been to Shaw's park dozens of times, but not since high school. It was a loop trail nearly two and a half miles long with just enough inclines and a couple sets of stairs which left you felling like you got some good exercise after you completed it. A creek ran through it, and part of the trail ran parallel to the water. The views were breathtaking. Warning signs were posted all over the trail alerting hikers to the dangers of wild animals in the area, encouraging them to stay on the marked path. Ashley rolled her eyes remembering the signs. Aside from a few common garden variety snakes and some frogs, the biggest animals you'd see here were rabbits and squirrels. This neck of the woods did have the highest number of bear attacks in the country, but the locals knew better.

"Just you wait," Jeff was saying. "The view is incredible."

Ashley exhaled loudly then quickly forced a smile his way. The last thing she wanted was to argue with him about her mood. She'd been looking forward to revisiting Shaw's Park from the moment he mentioned it earlier in the week, but he'd been going on and on about the view ever since she got in his car that morning. They'd never come out here together, but he did know she'd been out here many times in the past. He should understand she was well aware of the views the trails offered which made her think he was talking about something off the marked hike.

Between the three-quarter and one mile markers, there was a well beaten path on the left. It led uphill to a clearing where the view was said to be incredible. It overlooked the country side to the east, and according to friends of hers, the top of Ravenwood castle could be seen. No one went there for the view. It was a popular make out spot, or at least it had been in high school. Ashley never ventured off trail. She was terrified of Ravenwood. Five miles away from it while on a clearly marked hiking trail in a memorial park was the closest she dared to get.

Her friends all made fun of her. They called her a chicken. Called her a baby. That was because they didn't know; she never told them. The old Firebird sitting in her dad's garage, vintage. The envy of all her high school boyfriends had belonged to her late uncle. An uncle she'd never met. An uncle who supposedly died of a bear attack along Route 116. It had been fully restored by her dad, and there was no visible indication it had ever been wrecked. Her dad only drives it twice a year on Billy's birthday and the anniversary of his death.

They wouldn't have called her names and accused her of being afraid if they'd known the whole story. "I still am," she muttered under her breath.

"What was that?" Jeff asked.

Ashley looked up with wide eyes. She hadn't intended on saying that out loud. "I am ready." She hoped he hadn't caught her actual words.

Jeff clapped his hands and rubbed them together. "Great!" He jumped up and grabbed their trash, tossing it in the bin near their table. "Just got to grab one thing," he said, jogging back to his car.

She slowly walked away from the trail entrance to where he had headed as he pulled a backpack out of the back of the Civic. *'A backpack for a two and a half mile hike. Really?'*

"What's that?" Her eyebrow raised seeing her suspicions were accurate.

"Just a few things," he said, sliding the straps onto his shoulders. "It's good to be prepared."

"Like what?" she asked, forcing another smile as he walked over to her. *'Tell me there's a blanket, Jeff. I dare you.'*

"Oh, you know, a couple bottles of water and granola bars."

"Looks pretty full for just that."

"I brought a blanket too just in case," he added.

'Jerk.' Ashley focused on remaining calm. "A blanket?" Her anger surfaced as laughter. "For what?" Boys always thought they were pulling a fast one, and they never failed to underestimate their target. *'Say it, Jeff.'*

"It's a chilly day. The temperature's gonna drop near the water. I brought it in case you got cold."

'Sure you did, Jeff.'

"How sweet," she told him.

They set off on the trail with Jeff raving about the views again.

"Yes, I know. I've been here before," she reminded him. "I know all about the views of Shaw's Park," she added. It wasn't a lie. She did know about them even if she hadn't seen the ones off trail. It shut him up for the moment at least. She wondered if he was figuring out she knew exactly what he was planning. Maybe he was wondering if someone had already shown her these views. Maybe more than one someone had. She laughed at the thought.

"What's so funny?"

"Oh," Ashley stalled, scrambling to find a good cover. "I was thinking about when we got the sandwiches. That person in front of us in line. Their outfit!" She forced another laugh.

"Yeah," Jeff chuckled. "I had forgot about that."

When they reached the three-quarter mile marker, Ashley noticed Jeff slowed down his pace. It might have been just her imagination playing tricks on her since she'd been so certain she'd figured out what he was doing from the beginning. Ashley continued hiking without looking at him because if she saw him scanning the left side of the trail for the path, she wasn't sure she could control her outburst. As it was, she didn't know how she'd handle it when he suggested they should see where it led without dumping him on the spot. After all, she would need a ride home.

Ashley saw it before he did. With the recent rain, you wouldn't notice it if you didn't already know it was there. They started to hike past it. She never doubted what his true intentions had been, but for a brief moment, she thought he'd miss it, miss the opportunity to lead her up to a teenage make out area. Then as they were passing it, he stopped.

"What's this?" he asked. The surprise in his voice didn't come close to sounding real.

"What's what?" Ashley asked, not having to put much attempt in making the question sound believable given the muddy state of the ground.

"It looks like the start of another path here. Do you think the park is expanding its trails?"

'Oh my God!' Ashley screamed inside her head. *'How old are you?'* This might work on a teenager, but they were adults. The idea of going to a popular make out spot wasn't necessarily a bad one. College roommates were annoying and made having any privacy virtually impossible. Neither of them made enough

money at their part-time jobs to afford a room, and Jeff's old two door Civic made making out awkward and borderline painful. If they were going to take their relationship to the next level, they'd have to get creative. *'But this! Trying to trick me into sleeping with you? No, I don't think so.'* All he'd have to do is say, "If you're ready, I know a great secluded spot." She wouldn't have agreed to this one, but there are others.

"Let's check it out. It could be fun."

Ashley stared at him. She wanted to scream. She wanted to shout. She wanted to dump him. Mostly she wanted to throat punch him and walk back to the car while he lay on the ground gasping for breath. Instead, she shrugged in agreement. There was something within her stronger than her fear of Ravenwood, and it was the overwhelming desire to turn Jeff on, to take him to the brink of consummating their relationship before changing her mind because she's not ready. She had never considered herself that type of girl. It was something she'd never done, but you know what they say about desperate times. Jeff was deserving of desperate measures.

'Wow! Look at the view! I told you, didn't I?' She could already hear him, and it heated her with anger, picturing it playing out. *Jeff spread the blanket on the ground. Good thing he brought it, huh? They sit and chat for a bit, enjoying the scenery before he makes his move.*

She followed him not seeing any resemblance of a path after the first ten or fifteen steps, but she blindly trusted he knew where he was going. It was obvious she wasn't the first girl he had brought up here and probably not the first one he duped into it either. Disappointment crept over her clouding her mood to match the overcast skies. Their end was near. The break up would occur before the night was over even if he didn't have a clue. She had thought they were working toward developing something real, but this made her feel cheap, used, and no different from any other girl in his past.

One thing led to another, and they're lying spent on the blanket. The top of Ravenwood Inn, the thief of dreams, the bringer of nightmares, can be seen in the distance.

They hadn't been walking long, maybe twenty minutes when she checked her phone for the time, calculating when she'd be back. A few of her friends were going to a frat party that night, and she hoped to join them, seeing as how she'd be single. It shouldn't be much further. Everyone said it wasn't far off the marked trail, but 'wasn't far' wasn't an exact measurement.

None of it planned out in advance by Jeff, of course.

They continued walking and made it to the summit. They went down the other side and back again. They zigzagged this way and that. Ashley was paying closer attention to where they went. There was no path she could discern anywhere, muddied from the rain or otherwise.

It had been close to a half hour since she last checked her phone plus the approximate twenty minutes from leaving the trail until she first checked the time. Even by teenage standards, almost an hour didn't equal 'wasn't far.' They were lost.

Her heartrate quickened. This was the wrong area of the state to be lost in the woods. There was no need to panic, not yet. They couldn't have walked five miles in less than an hour. They couldn't be inside the property line of Ravenwood, but it was a definite possibility if they didn't find their way back soon.

"Jeff," she said.

He threw his hand out to stop her. "We're almost there," he said. "It's not far now."

"Where?" she asked. There was more anger cutting into her voice than she intended. "I thought this was a new path."

He glared at her and turned away. "That's right, and I'm taking us back to the old trail."

'Thank God,' she thought. She hurried her step to catch up with him then froze in place when she looked out over the ravine. A shiver rocked through her entire body. The grounds at Ravenwood had a ravine, and it wasn't necessarily contained inside the castle property. This could be a different one, but she wasn't sure if there were others in the area. Knowing it could be the one that ran through Ravenwood was enough to send her mind into overdrive, imagining what they might face at the mercy of the trees.

Ashley squeezed her eyes shut. *'You didn't walk five miles in under an hour. You're not at Ravenwood.'*

"You're cold," Jeff said.

When she opened her eyes, he had the backpack sitting on the ground, pulling the blanket from it.

"I saw you shiver." He draped it over her shoulders. She didn't refuse it, but she didn't exactly want it either. He handed her a bottle of water before zipping the bag closed and putting it on his back. "Might as well get it out while I had the bag open," he said.

He started walking again, and Ashley checked her phone, not for the time. There was no signal which is what she expected to see. They had to get to the car. Her dad had already lost a brother to Ravenwood. She couldn't bear the thought of him losing his only child to it as well.

They had been walking for hours. Jeff had stopped to relieve himself behind a tree for the second time when Ashley checked her phone again. She needed to go badly, but she would wet her pants before doing anything untoward. It wasn't because of a delicate nature, but because she didn't trust the trees.

She waited for him by the ravine. It was the fifth time she found herself staring into it. No matter which direction they walked or for how long, they would always find themselves being cut off by it. They weren't walking in circles. Nothing about this area was familiar. Even the ravine held different qualities and features than she had seen while staring into it the other times. Whether it was the same ravine or a different one didn't matter. It was Ravenwood.

Her eyes watered again as they did every time that name popped into her head. Tears stung the corners of her eyes, and she blinked rapidly trying to hold them back. This was not the time to panic. If she was going to make it out of the woods, she had to keep a clear head and stay focused.

Ashley had been doing what she could to protect herself. She tried to walk inside of Jeff's footprints. The recesses his shoes left in the mud made it easy for her to step exactly where he did. He had crumpled the water bottle, tossing it on the ground when he finished it. She quickly picked it up and had been carrying it ever since. If anyone was pissing off the woods today, it would be him.

He walked up behind her and asked, "Doing okay?"

It had taken him close to two hours, but he finally admitted they were lost. He hadn't spoken much since, but his voice had a kinder tone to it when he did.

"Yeah, but I'm getting hungry."

He nodded. "Me too." He set the backpack on the ground and reached inside, handing her a granola bar.

It was smashed flat as a pancake, but unopened, still edible. She ate it slowly, listening to the sounds her stomach made as it reacted. It wouldn't be near enough to fill her up. If anything, it would probably leave her feeling hungrier than she already was. Her stomach growled again, and she wondered if Jeff could hear it.

Jeff pulled out the only other thing left in the backpack, the other water bottle, and handed it to her. She put her wrapper and the empty bottle she'd been carrying inside the bag before he could zip it. When she went to unscrew the lid off the second bottle, she paused. It had already been opened and wasn't full, but this was the first time Jeff had taken it out of the bag. She held it in front of her one hand holding the bottle and one hand on the cap, staring at the water line. "Did you already get into this bottle?" she asked, knowing he hadn't.

"What?" His earlier anger reappeared in his voice. "I wouldn't do that, Ashley."

She held the bottle out to him. "So this must be Tori then, huh?"

They had dated last fall and well into the winter. Jeff had dumped her for Ashley. That's why the granola bars were smashed. They had been in the backpack in the car since the last time he took some girl out this way.

"Ohhh!" Ashley moaned loudly in disgust as the realization set in. She shook the blanket off her, and it fell to the ground. "Did you even wash that?"

"What are you talking about?" Jeff picked the blanket off

the ground, holding it out to her.

"Cut the crap, Jeff. You took me out here to trick me into going to the make out spot, and I get the feeling I'm not the first girl you pulled this with."

"I don't know what you're talking about," he said, offering the blanket to her again.

Ashley shook her head.

"Fine," he said, shoving the blanket into the bag. "You might not have noticed since you were wrapped up in this, but the temperature's been dropping." He put the bag on his shoulders then blew into his cupped hands and rubbed them together for emphasis.

"If you're so cold, why don't *you* wear the blanket?"

Jeff glared at her sideways.

"Is it because you know what stains are on it?"

"Let's just get back to the car," he said.

"Agreed." Ashley took a step away, and a twig snapped beneath her feet. She froze. Her eyes widened. Goosebumps popped up on her arms, and the little hairs on the back of her neck stood on end. *'Oh, God, no,'* she thought. "I am so sorry. I didn't mean to cause you any harm. Please forgive me. I'm lost," she said quietly.

"What's wrong with you?"

Ashley stared at him too busy concentrating on controlling an already full bladder to focus on forming anymore thoughts into words.

"We're not in Ravenwood," he scoffed. He reached for the nearest tree branch and shook it violently. If he was trying to snap it off, it didn't give. He turned his attention to a small bush growing near the edge of the ravine, grabbing hold and uprooting it entirely before throwing it over the side.

"You better pray we're not," she told him.

"I can't believe you're terrified of an urban legend," he said, unzipping the bag and dumping the trash out.

"I can't believe you're not," she whispered to herself.

Jeff threw the granola wrappers and empty water bottle into the ravine. The bottle made it, but the wrappers caught the breeze and flew back, landing on the ground behind him. Ashley walked away, not wanting to be guilty by association more than what she already might be held accountable.

"You're going the wrong way, Ash," Jeff yelled after her.

She stopped and looked at him, pointing to the sky where the sun had conveniently peeked out behind a cloud. "The sun sets in the west, Jeff," she said, and then pointed in the direction she had been heading. "That is east. That is Dunberry Road. That is safety."

"Suit yourself," he said, preparing to walk in the opposite direction. In a mocking voice he added, "Remember if the trees get you, there won't be anyone who will hear your cries for help."

Ashley walked away from him. Each step was deliberate and careful. Every couple minutes, she'd repeat her mantra. "I'm sorry. I don't mean to hurt you. I'm lost. Please forgive me."

It took no more than ten minutes for her feet to touch pavement. The entrance to Shaw's Park was twenty yards down the road to her left, and she headed toward it. One of the best things about the park was the facilities were indoors with running water.

Jeff's car was the only vehicle left in the parking lot. She tried calling his phone to tell him he was close to the park, but it went straight to voice mail. It would be dusk soon, and it would be ticketed. After three nights, it would be towed. That would be Monday. He would miss classes that day and be a no call, no show at work. She wondered how long it would be until he was reported as a missing person. It wouldn't be her who made the call. She couldn't do that to her father. She could never let him find out how close she came to following in her uncle's footsteps.

Ashley felt better after using the restroom until she glanced at Jeff's car again, feeling torn about doing the right thing. Although honestly, an adult isn't considered a missing person this quickly. Would they even take the report seriously? *'Yeah,'* she thought. *'They probably would being this close to Ravenwood, but they wouldn't do much about it.'*

A police car pulled into the lot, and Ashley watched as the officer parked the car facing her. He stepped out of the vehicle. "On your way out?" The officer pointed to Jeff's car. "I was going to lock the gate a little early tonight what with the storm's rolling in."

"Well," Ashley said, biting her lower lip. "I am, but that's my ex-boyfriend's car."

"Ex-boyfriend?"

"He tried making a move on the trail, so I came back," she explained. It wasn't far from the truth. "I was getting ready to call a friend for a ride."

"And what if he shows up before your ride does?" the cop asked. "Where do you live?"

"Wheaton," Ashley told him. Actually she lived on campus in the city, but she could go to her dad's. It was closer anyway.

The cop opened the backdoor of the squad car, "Hop in. I'll give you a ride."

"Do me a favor," he said, turning out onto Dunberry Road. "Send him a text letting him know you found a ride home. It'll save a missing person call when he makes it back to the car and sees you're nowhere around."

"Good idea." Ashley pulled out her phone and sent the text to Jeff. It would hold up if she was questioned after someone noticed he was missing. She glanced in the direction of the park and wondered if Jeff had already learned for himself there was no one around to hear his cries for help.

Chapter Eleven
Weaver Women

Rosemary sat at her desk after her morning walk and finished the letter she'd been working on for the better part of a week. The grounds crew who wasn't out when she left were hard at work upon her return. She tried to avoid being seen and left early in the morning to visit the clearing before anyone, but the overnight security guard was around. They had an understanding. He kept his mouth shut about her comings and goings, and in return, she paid him a handsome shift differential for working thirds.

Her daughter Edit handled the shift on his days off. She was the only Weaver woman old enough to do the job and young enough to handle the hours. Edit always worked the overnight guard detail as needed. She even worked two weeks straight once to cover his vacation. They all had to make a contribution to running the inn, but she didn't do it without voicing her objections. No conversation could be had with her that didn't involve complaining. As soon as Edit's daughter Lucinda turned eighteen, the minimum age posted for the position, Edit would force it on her. "Happy Birthday! Now, go to work."

Movement on one of the camera angles on the small television screen sitting on the corner of her desk caught her eye. A young guest was an apparent early riser. He stood not far from the trail entrance and looked around at the groundskeepers tending to the flowers in the courtyard. Rosemary inhaled deeply and waited. The man left and walked the path through the flower garden instead.

Rosemary exhaled sharply, and she realized how disappointed she was. *'Not disappointed.'* She rolled her eyes. The guests who followed the posted trail times were just as likely to break the rest of the rules as someone who preferred to exercise early. The trees didn't care what time people ventured into their boundaries, so long as they left the woods alone. Those hours were set because it was the time frame she had staff to patrol the path, not because the trees didn't like being woken up early. The real cause for the rules was to prevent as much litigation as possible.

'Supposedly patrolled it.' There was staff working the grounds who would respond to any screams if the sounds made their way out of the woods, but no one actually walked the area like guests were told. The inn couldn't afford what someone would demand to be paid to do that job.

Rosemary stuffed the letter and the other forms into an envelope and began addressing it. Halfway through writing the address, she dropped her pen and shoved the envelope away from her. She gritted her teeth and covered the mess with her desk planner, not wanting to be disgusted by the sight of it any longer.

The lady wasn't at the clearing this morning. She hadn't shown for quite a long time, and Rosemary guessed it's because she was unhappy. The last few times Rosemary had seen her the lady was concerned about the lack of foot traffic in the woods.

Locals still came out from time to time. There was a joker in every crowd who wanted to prove Ravenwood was nothing more than a scary campfire story to tell children, and that person usually wound up the subject of future campfire tales. It was happening less often. The woods depended on tourism to satiate them, and it was lacking.

Vacations were changing. People weren't driving as much. They were flying and not to western Massachusetts either. The popular destinations were the large cities, the beaches, and whatever parks the man with a mouse had dreamt up. Family expenses were growing, but they were trying hard to maintain appearances. They stayed in these cheap chain motels right off the highway. No one wanted to spend the extra green on a fancy European place. Their biggest revenue came from celebrations like anniversaries.

If business didn't pick up soon, she might be the Weaver girl who lost the property. Rosemary covered her face with her hands, taking a few deep breaths to clear her mind. That wasn't an option. She closed her eyes, moved the calendar out of the way, and felt around on her desk until she found the envelope. If only she could finish addressing it with her eyes closed, it might not hurt as bad.

They had suffered enough. Her Yanyo Rozalia still couldn't walk down the sidewalks of the nearby towns without people running into traffic to cross the street. People cursed her, and worse, sometimes they spat at her. Yanyo was believed to be a gypsy when she first arrived, but now the family were mostly considered to be witches. None of them could leave. They were trapped on this property, destined to run the family business with no help from whatever man they married. *A man who was awfully hard to find.'* Most aren't forward thinking enough to accept a woman who wants to keep her name. That was her Yanyo's doing.

Rosemary shook her head and stood up from her desk. Her interviewee for the receptionist job would be here soon, and she wanted another cup of coffee before the young woman arrived. It would be a waste of time. Hiring relatives or friends never worked out. The tips and tricks employees learned to soothe their time on the property were passed along to the newcomer before they filled out the employment application. There was very little fear when they knew what to expect and how to deal with it. Ravenwood needed fresh blood, but serious applicants were few and far between.

The break room was filled with smoke, and it gagged her when she opened the door. She never minded the smell of cigarettes or pipe tobacco, but better ventilation would be nice. There was no room in the budget for that anytime soon.

The glass carafe was on the warming plate of the electric coffee maker with barely enough coffee to cover the bottom of it. Rosemary rinsed it out and prepared another pot to brew. "Most of these guys don't have one like this at home yet to know how to make a good pot anyway." She looked around quickly, making sure no one had come in behind her. *It's true though.'*

While she waited for the coffee to brew, she stared at the picture on the wall of her grandparents. It was her favorite picture of them. They looked so happy. Joseph Weaver had died just shy of two years ago. He had lived a long life but was still too young to be gone. Rozalia, on the other hand, didn't look a day over fifty, and she was a year older than her husband. *'No wonder they think we're witches.'*

Rosemary didn't wait for the entire pot to brew. She poured a cup from what was ready and took it back to her desk. Her grandparents went through hell after they reappeared out of thin air and built this castle. That photograph was probably one of the last times their smiles were genuine.

It's why the Weaver name must be maintained. Yanyo Rozalia insists on showing this state who her husband was and what he was capable of achieving.

"He was a great man." Rosemary sighed, thinking about him. "Unlike Wilbur." She glanced at the base of the ring finger on her left hand. The white line where she once wore a wedding band was still faint and probably only noticeable if you knew it was there. By the end of the summer, she'd have enough sun to rid herself of the mark permanently.

It'd be a solid plan if the business was actually successful. Rosemary picked up the envelope off her desk she'd been fidgeting with all morning. "Is this what I'm reduced to?" she shook her head.

A couple minutes later, the envelope was sealed and almost ready to post. *'Ripley's.'* She silently asked her grandfather to forgive her for what she was reduced to for the sake of the inn.

When the large envelope came in the mail, Rosemary had been excited. A new television show, or a rebooted one, highlighting the strange and unusual was the perfect place to showcase Ravenwood. If this inn could be featured on television, business would boom for six months, maybe a year. The uptick in revenue could boost their paid ads, and salvation might finally be within arm's reach.

Only there was no television show.

There was only a comic book.

Rosemary let the envelope drop to the desk again. There wasn't a choice. Free advertising was still advertising, but that wasn't all. Ripley's was going to feature the inn and the property with or without her consent. The letter was more or less a complimentary head's up. However, if she wanted a specific tale to be told, she was welcome to submit it in her own words. That was the only spin she could control, choosing the right angle to pique a reader's interest without scaring them away from the eastern part of the States for life.

There had to be another way, but if there was, it was lost to her. The one question she never dared ask the lady, her Yanyo, or anyone, was, "What happens to us if we lose it all?"

Some questions are better left unanswered. They can't leave, not without permission, and not for long. Ravenwood wouldn't let them walk away and start over somewhere new. The inn couldn't fail because their lives were connected to it. The Weavers didn't spend five decades surviving in this pitiful existence, offering sacrifices to mystic powers in the trees they barely understood, only to have their lineage abruptly come to an end because Rosemary couldn't draw in enough guest to pay the overhead. What would the woods do to them if that came to pass?

"What was that?" Rosemary shot up straight in her chair. There was no noise, but something happened. Something was different. She glanced at the monitor, but saw nothing questionable. There was no movement on the trail at all near as she could tell.

The trees were growing restless. Perhaps they had called out. It wasn't a noise, not anything audible. She could sense them. Any emotion they portrayed could be felt if you had a connection to them like her family did. It was beyond time she gave them what they wanted.

She reached into the middle desk drawer and pulled out the remainder of her sheet of stamps. The perforations had always pained her. She usually ripped more stamps than she used. The scissors were in the drawer too, and she cut along the edges of the stamp where the design holes were to make separating them easier. Once one was cut out, she put the sheet and the scissors away and licked the back of the stamp. She placed it on the corner of the envelope and pressed hard for several seconds making sure it would stick.

The beakers containing various colored liquids on the chemistry themed stamp looked cool when Rosemary bought them. Science was her favorite subject. If she wasn't born into a life sentence at Ravenwood, it would be the field she'd have pursued. Now, the stamp reminded her of a life that wasn't truly hers.

"Thirteen cents," she grumbled. "And they're already wanting to raise the cost again to fifteen!" It really was no wonder people could only afford rooms at the cheap chains when they traveled.

A chill rocked down her spine, and Rosemary shivered. It was definitely the woods. She scanned the camera angles on the television screen again, but there was no movement. If someone had gone off trail, they could be far from the nearest camera by now.

It never got easier. Honestly, there was little more she could do. Signs were posted. Tales of the woods were commonplace for a hundred-mile radius if not farther. This property had made the news more than the state of the economy which seemed to be the only other thing anyone was discussing anymore. There had already been mention of Ravenwood in certain paranormal circles. The word was out there. It was like telling people the sky was blue, but they had to look up to see for themselves.

Still, it did nothing to ease her guilt. Every missing person, every abandoned vehicle, every new item added to the branches in the clearing like souvenirs was another mark on her soul. Rosemary was confident she'd be held accountable for the lives lost one day.

Whatever she was feeling was growing stronger. *'Maybe it's all for the best.'* She picked up the envelope once more and walked it to the reception desk to drop it in the basket. The mailman refused to set foot on the property. At shift change, one of her employees would drive it to the post office when they took the deposit to the bank. They'd considered putting a mailbox along 116, but it'd be too tempting to the teenagers looking for mischief. Ravenwood's body count might be in a slump currently, but it was still too high for Rosemary to invite the deaths of countless teenage boys to stain her soul.

As she walked through the office door, she felt the energy surge. It wasn't pleasant, but she was used to it. What most people viewed as grim or eerie was a good sign in these parts. It meant the woods were happy. A good day at the inn meant some poor soul was suffering. The Ripley's comic book could only help their reach, and the trees were being rejuvenated.

The strange sensation continued to intensify. Rosemary stood behind the desk with the letter in her hand, trying to remember the last time it was this strong. She was drawing a blank.

"Mrs. Weaver?"

The voice broke through her thoughts, and she stared at Bev, the young woman working the desk. "What was that?" she asked.

Bev reached her hand out. "Do you want me to take that for you, Mrs. Weaver?"

Rosemary looked down. The letter she needed to mail had temporarily escaped her mind, and she was surprised to see anything in her hands. "Oh, yes," she said. "Thank you."

"You feel it too." The words came out as a statement, not a question.

It shocked Rosemary. "I didn't realize you could sense them."

"Them?" Bev looked confused. "I don't know what you mean by them. I was talking about the cloud of dread that descends sometimes, this feeling of foreboding."

'What would foreboding feel like to someone who's only known that feeling their entire life?' she wondered.

"There's your interview." Bev nodded toward the door.

Rosemary looked out the window and watched the car careen its way off the lane and into the lot. The feeling grew. *'Excitement. That's what it feels like.'*

'No.' She composed herself. *'The trees are excited, not me.'*

"I'm going to use the ladies room before the interview," Rosemary said to her employee. "Show her to my desk. Have her wait there."

Bev nodded.

Rosemary walked through the office door and grabbed her steno-book and pen from her desk. She hurried to the break room and pulled the large trash bin over to prop open the door. It was in part to air out some of the smoke, but also to watch for the woman she was to interview arrive. The feeling continued to grow. The trees wanted her.

'No, it can't be her that's causing this. She'd know everything. Surely, she'd have been told.'

The excitement, or dread, or whatever it was reached its peak and held steady. Rosemary watched as the young woman sat at the desk. Her fear could be felt in the break room.

She slipped into the hall and walked softly toward her, hoping the woman wouldn't notice her. The woman froze solid and sat stiff, paralyzed with terror. When Rosemary approached her, she dropped her notebook and pen on the desk. The woman jumped and almost fell from her chair, catching herself but sending the chair toppling to the floor. The sound of the trees shaking their branches as if the leaves were clapping in delight could be faintly heard. The rustling outside died down, and the anticipation began to build again. They truly did want her.

"Hello, Alice," she said, extending her hand before taking her seat. "I'm Mrs. Rosemary Weaver. You may call me Mrs. Weaver."

She rushed through the interview, reciting the questions from memory, and barely attending the answers. Her lips stayed pursed. It was the only way to stop herself from smiling. What luck!

This woman was horrified. The reasons why she'd look for a job at a place which caused her such fright weren't important. There was a story to it she was sure, but not one that mattered.

It couldn't work out any better. It was a win for everyone.

The woman would get a job which she must be in desperate need of getting to torture herself like this. Rosemary would finally fill the long vacated second shift front desk position. *'And the trees!'*

Ravenwood could feed off her energy and be sustained. It might not last long, but they'd be content for a while. There'd be no blood shed added to Rosemary's guilt today.

When the woman left, she practically ran out of the office. Rosemary's laughter flowed when the door shut behind her. This was what she needed. Things were looking up. She eyed the clock, estimating how long it'd take Alice to get home.

It wasn't set in stone yet. Alice would have to accept the job offer, but she felt certain she would. The fear she exhibited meant she needed the job badly. *'Why else would she show up for the interview? ... Because someone forced her to come.'*

Rosemary dug the application out of the file in her desk and called the number listed as fast as her fingers could dial. She prayed she didn't mess up the number on the rotary. If Alice drove fast, and she probably did to get away from here, she could already be home.

She dragged the dial for the last number and waited. There was a ring. *'I hope I didn't wait too long.'* It rang again. *'Why didn't I think of this sooner?'*

The line connected, and a woman's voice said, "Hello?"

Rosemary considered hanging up. "Alice?"

"No, this is her mother. Alice isn't at home. May I take a message?"

She slumped back in her chair thankful for all the miracles happening around her today. "Yes, that would be wonderful. My name is Mrs. Weaver. I'm calling to offer her the position at

Ravenwood."

Chapter Twelve
Chasing Ghosts

Ryan sat in his office waiting for Mr. Meyers to end his phone call. It could be construed as unprofessional to indulge such distractions during an interview. He sighed, hearing from the one side of the conversation he had access to it would be at least another few minutes. He had shown every respect including addressing him with a title even though he looked barely out of college which would make him at least a decade younger.

His office was the garage, but the goal was to rent his own space one day. That had been the dream since he first got his feet wet in ghost hunting while in college, and within the month, it would finally be achieved. Luckily, he married a woman who loved him enough to support him during the years he wasn't making much of a living off it.

The garage had been converted years ago when he outgrew the basement. It had been in the corner of the downstairs when he set up shop for his business originally. He used a cubicle divider he salvaged when the company his wife works for remodeled, separating his corner from the family room which took up most of the remainder of the space.

Glancing back up at the reporter from Para-News magazine, Ryan saw him mouth the word, "Sorry."

It sounded important. Ryan tried not to eavesdrop too much, but he caught key words like, *test results*, and *second opinion*.

Twenty years ago last January, he changed his major to psychology. His parents didn't mind that career choice even if they were a bit surprised. The following June when he spent his summer traveling the country assisting various self-proclaimed psychics, mediums and ghost hunters, his parents chalked it up to youthful expression and convinced themselves it was a quirky hobby he was getting out of his system.

He did it again the next summer and was often contacted to assist during his senior year. A few cases he turned down, but he still missed enough days of class to make graduation uncertain at one point. That part his parents never learned about because he grabbed any letters from the school before they saw the day's mail.

When he forego all typical routes for a psychology degree and created a ghostbusting business as his dad called it, he was surprised they didn't cut all ties with him. Sometimes he wishes he named the business "Boo-vies" just to get under his dad's skin. As it was, his dad spent years trying to talk him out of changing it because he used the family name. "Chasing's Occult World" was what he called himself in the beginning. It's been "Chasing Ghosts" for over a decade, and his dad still wasn't happy. His parents took to introducing him as a therapist early on, leaving off the part of how his patients are spirits. It's getting harder for them to hide from it with his recognition growing. Ryan can barely go anywhere without someone pointing and taking pictures. Even with his success, they're still ashamed.

The phone call was ending, and Ryan reached into his pocket and fidgeted with a key. He had taken it out of its hiding spot before the man from the magazine arrived. There had been countless interviews over the years, but he'd always kept certain pieces of information to himself. He had decided today would be the day he laid it all out in the open and share what sparked his interest in the most mysterious woods in the country. The magazine was paying him handsomely for the interview. Well, they were enticing him to free up some time was more like it since he was booked into next year. With that dollar amount, it was only right they get the scoop.

Mr. Meyers sat back down apologizing for the interruption. "Thank you again for your time. I have one last topic I'd like to cover if that's alright?"

Ryan chuckled quietly. He called it. Most people brought it up eventually. It wasn't hard to figure out what was coming next.

"You know what I'm about to ask." Meyers pushed the record button and opened his notebook. "Ravenwood. You have established yourself as the leading expert which is no small feat considering its popularity in the field, but it is remarkable for someone who's never been there."

"I have been to Ravenwood many times."

"Fair. For someone who's never conducted paranormal research there. Better?"

Ryan grinned and said, "That's not entirely true either."

The reporter gave him a look that begged him to continue. "I'm all ears."

He went on to recount how he and his wife had stayed there over a dozen times. They would spend a weekend each trip, and he'd do what he could while he was there to investigate without being detected. He'd bring a camera and recorder each time, and he added an EMF meter to his later visits. None of his attempts were successful, but he continued to try until one of his videos went viral. Once his face was out there in the public eye, he was banned from returning by the owner Lucy.

Ryan chuckled silently. The one thing in this world Lucinda Weaver might despise more than Ravenwood was being called Lucy. He learned that the hard way, and referred to her by the nickname ever since being thrown out of his room at two in the morning.

"Not successful. Are you saying you didn't find any evidence of the supernatural at Ravenwood?"

"No, not at all. It's all around. Some people are more sensitive to spirits than others, but I'd be surprised to meet someone who can honestly claim they didn't experience anything while there."

As he spoke, he pulled out an assortment of pictures he had selected ahead of time. Most were orbs. There were orbs for days in these shots. He led up to the better pictures of full apparitions. Even these had varying degrees of clarity, but the best was taken in a hallway of the manor. Everyone jumps to the conclusion he captured an image of Rozalia who was the original owner of the inn, but he wasn't convinced. If the image was clearer, he'd be able to say without a shadow of a doubt, but his gut told him it was a woman named Alice, one of the many employees who worked at Ravenwood until their death.

"This," Ryan said, pulling up a file on his computer. "This is my favorite."

He played the video of a tree not far from the walking trail on the property. The facial features etched into the trunk was more than pareidolia. It almost looked professionally carved. "This is Earl."

"Earl?" Meyers asked.

Ryan shrugged. "There was a girl on the trail that day. I didn't know who she was at the time, but she saw me studying this tree, this face. She told me his name."

Meyers looked like he wasn't sure if he was joking around or not.

"I thought Earl was as good a name as any, and I went with it. Then I learned who she was."

"Who was she?"

He lifted a finger to his lips to silence him. The show was about to start.

They watched sixteen full minutes of grainy footage. Ryan would've given anything to bring a better camera, a better anything with him on his trips to Ravenwood, but he had to be secretive.

Ryan asked precisely twelve questions to the tree, allowing time for answers to each one. He also carried a voice recorder with him that day, but what he captured on film far exceeded his expectations. After each question, the tree moaned and shook. That's not the right word, but it swayed without the slightest breeze to move it. Every other tree in frame didn't flick a leaf, but Earl was active.

The tape neared the end with Ryan's final question. "Are you in pain, Earl?"

The agonizing groans that played on the video still made goosebumps appear on Ryan's arms. From the corner of his eye, he saw the shiver that rocked through Meyers. Ask a hundred people and get a hundred different answers. Ryan Chasing was convinced whoever Earl was, he was forever trapped in a tree to experience eternity in utter torture.

With a few seconds remaining, Ryan paused the video. He wanted the last image to remain on screen, and if the video finished, it would fade to black.

"Wait," Meyers mumbled.

Ryan lowered his eyes to his desk. No one watched the video without seeing what had already been deeply embedded into his mind. The images of Earl woke him with a fright more times than he could remember. As a little child, he was afraid of snakes and spiders, but grew to love them. Over the years, his fears changed course often from failing a test at school to being rejected by the girl who made his heart skip a beat. Ravenwood always held an apprehension, a caution label that warned to proceed with care. Since he first watched the playback, his biggest fear has been dying at the whim of those trees.

This would be the first location he set up for investigation once he was allowed on the property. It would happen, and it was more than a positive outlook urging the thought. Every owner had allowed the curious to come out with cameras and their crew to curb their morbid fascination, film for a segment or do an article. It brought business, brought income to the family.

Not Lucy. She was the one who snubbed her heritage where Ravenwood was concerned. The property had suffered as a result. He might not be allowed to come back, but he had many colleagues in the field who weren't banned. It was in desperate need for upkeep and maintenance.

In his gut, he knew Lorelei would change things once she was in charge. He saw it on her face in those brief moments when they spoke. She was a believer, but it was more than that. Lorelei had the respect for Ravenwood it demanded. She would do what was necessary, but he also saw her passion for the place. He had to believe she'd want the same answers he sought to find.

"Did the face change? It couldn't have. Could it? Can I see the beginning again?"

There was no need to replay it. Ryan minimized the video and pulled up the image he had ready. It was a split screen of Earl, one image from the start and one from the end side by side. It was clearly the same face, still Earl, but the expression was different. The change was so gradual it wasn't easy to detect while watching, even with knowing to pay attention, but it happened nonetheless. Earl was just as mournful, and his face grotesquely skewed in a permanent expression of pain. The shape of the mouth had changed. The tree, or the spirit trapped inside it, was trying to speak.

"That's not possible." After several minutes of staring at the screen with his eyes darting between the two images, Meyers straightened his posture resolved to not believe.

Add it to the list of what Ryan had anticipated. He told Meyers the same as he'd said to everyone who'd seen it. "I'd be happy to have any expert of your choosing review the tape. It hasn't been altered."

Meyers didn't question it again, but continued to intently look at the image. His face was hardened like he was a stern skeptic, but his eyes told another story. They were filled with a fear. It was the type of fright that once gripped onto the soul, it never unleashes its hold.

The interviewer shivered again, and it broke the spell. He shook his head and glanced at his notes. "Where were we?"

'True to form,' Ryan thought. *'When faced with something we can't explain and aren't well equipped to handle, we choose to ignore it.'*

"The girl?" Meyers asked after a moment. "Who was she?"

Ryan's eyes twinkled relishing the information he was about to drop. This would be a pleasant distraction from Earl after all. Most of his interviews end with him feeling like he had attended a funeral. "Her name was Lorelei... Lorelei Weaver."

The sudden intake of air scraping over Meyer's teeth as he gasped was music to Ryan's ears. Every Weaver woman since Rozalia set foot in this country had been willing to do interviews focusing on the occult appeal of the property until Lucy came along. She looked down her nose at everything associated with her family name. A more private woman had never existed. Every detail was kept under wraps including her daughter.

Staff had let the word out over the years that an heir did exist, but not much more was known, aside from her name. She rarely left the inn's grounds.

"You actually saw her?" Meyers was impressed.

Ryan nodded slowly. "I only wish I'd realized who she was at the time, but if I had hounded Lorelei with questions, I would've been kicked off the property a lot sooner than I was," he laughed.

That wasn't the whole truth either, but a secret is only a secret until it's shared. It wouldn't be long until Lorelei took over the property. Once that happened, things would return to how they were. Documentaries, ghost hunters, articles, all of it would be welcomed back to Ravenwood, and Chasing Ghosts would have the first crack at it.

"When was this exactly?"

"Close to five years ago. She was probably about fifteen at the time, give or take."

Meyers shook his head and smiled. Setting eyes on the youngest Weaver woman was almost as difficult as catching Bigfoot. He glanced at his watch and inhaled sharply. "I apologize. I hadn't realized how late it was. Just a couple more questions if you have time."

"Shoot."

"Would you elaborate then? What do you mean these trips were unsuccessful? From what you've shown me, I would call your time there a praiseworthy feat."

This is where he lost everybody. What he would say next wouldn't be included when the interview appeared in the magazine. If any of it did get inked, it would be only to mock him and his theories. "I didn't get the evidence I wanted."

"Evidence? Of ghosts? Spirit activity? What you showed me was a great deal of proof that Ravenwood is haunted."

"It'd be hard to find someone who didn't believe Ravenwood was haunted. Even the fiercest skeptic would waiver after a few minutes in those trees. How many people have died, or disappeared and presumed dead, in that area during the last century? The lore surrounding it goes back before the first settlers arrived. Of course, it's haunted."

"Then what were you hoping to find?" Meyers looked genuinely curious. He was probably expecting a specific unsolved case, maybe something with a personal tie to Ryan.

Ryan braced his hands on the edge of his desk and pushed back until his arms were straight. The bruise on his index finger was almost healed leaving a nasty greenish yellow mark in its place. He stared at it while trying to talk himself out of what he already knew he was going to do. *'Don't say it. He'd buy it if you said you only meant you wanted to do a full investigation with all of your equipment.'*

"The dream is to discover the source fueling the power of Ravenwood."

Meyers was visibly confused, and he repeated the words quietly hoping they'd make more sense. "The source? Are you meaning the source of the paranormal activity?"

"In a word, yes."

"Then that would be the spirits." Meyers laughed and looked like he must've misheard something Ryan said.

"Beyond that." He leaned in closer to the interviewer and folded his arms on his desk. "The ghosts are what we see and to an extent, for some, what we feel. How did they get there?"

"They died," Meyers said, acting like he wasn't enjoying the game anymore. He folded his notebook and was about to end the recording.

"But how did they die?"

Meyers eyed him sharply then shook his head with a chuckle.

He was losing him, but he had to keep pushing. "There's a force in those woods, something far stronger than ghosts, regardless of how plentiful those may be."

"A force?" Meyers packed away his notebook in his bag, turned off the recorder and added it as well. He was acting like he couldn't leave fast enough.

Ryan couldn't stifle his laugh any longer. Interviewers will discuss ghosts, hauntings, EMF's, residual hauntings and poltergeists until they run out of breath, but think you're crazy if you mention the existence of a driving force behind all of that. "Yes," he said, shaking Meyers' extended hand. "Something runs the place, and it's not the Weavers."

Meyers muttered a goodbye and set his sights on the door. It shut a little too loudly when he left.

He pulled his cell phone out of his top drawer where he stashed it before the interview. A text from his wife was on the screen, and he laughed hard. "Don't do it," she said.

"Too late." He replied to the message then took the key out of his pocket. Meyers wasn't the one either. He flipped the key around in his fingers, wondering if he'd ever meet someone he could trust with the insight he had.

He locked the door on the garage in case Meyers returned for something he forgot before unlocking the bottom desk drawer and returning the key to his pocket. There was a large black box inside which he placed on the desk. Two combinations were needed to open it then he lifted the lid. An old hobo style bag laid on top, and he carefully set it on his desk. The contents of it could be recited in his sleep, including the recitation of every journal entry.

Another smaller box was at the bottom, and he lifted it out, and opened it. The old Martel reel to reel was inside, and he pulled the power cord out and plugged it in before sitting back down. Ryan rubbed his hands together nervously. His heart rate was skyrocketing as it always had when looking at these items. From the moment he acquired them the summer after his freshman year of college, they've both excited and frightened him.

He pulled the recorder out of the bag and rewound the tape for a few seconds. There were copies of everything stored safely in other places, not from fear of thieves as much as he worried he'd one day run the recordings down. He pressed play while he pulled a newspaper article out of the bag. It was the one thing he added to the lot himself, but he liked having the face to put with the tape. Crackling noises came through the speaker, but they weren't the standard dead air pops an older generation was used to hearing.

The crackling became louder until his mind convinced himself he could feel the heat of the flames on his face. Then came the screams.

As hard as it was, he also listened until there was nothing but silence left on the recording. He felt like it was out of respect for the dead, but not everyone would agree.

Once he was finished, he put the recorder back and turned his attention to the reel to reel. It was time to listen to the Lady again.

Chapter Thirteen
The Shortcut

"What's wrong with it?" Mandy asked.

Erin shrugged and rubbed her temples. "Heck if I know."

"Where are we? Are we close to a town?" Mandy looked back and forth down the country highway nervously. This trip had been a bad idea from the first mention of it. Mandy had tried to talk her friends out of it. There wasn't a reason she could give them except it didn't sit right with her. They made fun of her feelings even if they wound up being mostly true. That's why they were on this trip anyway. The girls had joked around about Mandy being a witch since her creepy feelings began when they were still in grade school. They didn't have the money for Florida, so they decided to road trip their senior spring break to Salem instead.

"What's the matter? Don't think you can make it if dinner's late?" Claire teased, elbowing Erin gently. The three girls giggled at her.

Her premonition style feelings weren't the only thing she was teased about by them. The extra twenty-five pounds she carried around her middle made her the fat friend. While they hated it when she used that word to describe herself, they took every opportunity to harass her about her weight. She would've stayed home, but she'd have spent the week by herself in her room with no other friends to hang out with until they returned.

Missy had been studying the map she spread over the hood of the car. "We're going to have to walk," she said, folding it up.

"How far?" Mandy raised her arm to check her watch, but caught herself. She brought her hand up to scratch her shoulder instead, hoping no one could tell what she meant to do. They'd just ask if she was late for supper.

"Not sure. Five miles, maybe more. We have to head back to that town we just passed through." Missy put the map back in the car and grabbed her purse. "Ready?"

'Appleton.' Mandy had wanted to buy snacks at the service station where they filled up the tank, but the girls didn't give her a moment alone. She could've taken something into the restroom on the side of the building to eat without them seeing. She had originally packed food for the road trip, but Claire was relentless about her eating too much causing her to leave it behind. Now she was starving, trying to talk over the sound of her stomach growling so the rest of them couldn't hear it.

Missy crossed the road and stared at the woods. "We'd save time if we cut through the trees. It's a shortcut."

"How so?" Erin walked up next to her. The two of them typically called the shots.

"The way the road curved around and out until the straightaway a few minutes back. It'd add time to our walk," Missy explained. She turned to Claire and Mandy. "The shortest distance between two points is a straight line, and Appleton is that way." She pointed with her arm to the trees.

"We could get picked up by a car on the road though." Claire suggested and glanced at Mandy with a small nod like she wanted back up.

"Yeah. What if we get lost? How do we know where to go?"

Erin laughed at her. "Don't worry, Mandy. You'll survive the longest without food of all of us."

The girls laughed at her again. "You know we love you," Claire said, draping an arm over Mandy's shoulders.

'Love to put me down is more like it.' Mandy smiled at her. "It's all good fun. I know."

"There are no cars." Missy walked over to Claire. "Haven't seen a soul since we been on this road. See the weeds growing in the cracks along the pavement?" Missy pointed at various spots near them. "This road is not well traveled. And all we have to do, Mandy, is keep the sun on that side of us." Missy pointed to where the sun hung in the sky. "We'll be in Appleton in no time."

A shiver ran down Mandy's spine, and goosebumps popped up on her arms. *'A soul? Why did I react to that?'*

"Fine, but you owe me." Claire didn't like to get dirty. A walk through the woods was akin to torture for her.

"Good." Missy clapped her hands together. "Let's get going."

"Class of '86!" Erin screamed throwing her arms straight overhead. She had been yelling it for everything they did since the school year began. It had grown annoying by Halloween.

'Nice of her to make sure I was okay with this.' Mandy brought up the rear. When they entered the woods, the temperature dropped. It was from the shade of the trees, but

it reminded her of a tomb. She couldn't shake the feeling something was coming.

Missy led the group using Erin's backpack to beat down any branches or brush in their way. There was very little light seeping in through the tops of the trees, and Mandy wasn't sure how Missy would be able to keep track of the direction they should head. She didn't say anything about it. Claire was teasing Erin about a hole a branch put in her shirt, exposing bare skin on her back where she had a mole. The longer the brunt of the jokes were off her the better.

The branch that attacked her was now a pretend sword Erin was using to strike every tree they passed. None of them believed her when she said the branch suddenly spun back and hit her without anything moving it, but she insisted she was assaulted. She was just messing around, but she kept up the act like it was serious.

"C'mon, Mandy! Keep up!" Missy hollered from the front of the line a few minutes into their trek.

Mandy picked up her pace. She wasn't more than five feet behind Claire as it was, not like she was going to lose them anytime soon, and she would make sure to keep them in her sights.

"Maybe you should slow down." Claire yelled out to Missy.

Mandy was relieved someone else said it, but surprised it was Claire. She had been complaining since her first step off the pavement about how gross the woods were and how much it stunk. The fresh air was a welcome relief to Mandy who'd been stuck in the backseat inhaling the perfume Claire poured on like she bathed in it since they left.

"You know Mandy has a lot more weight to carry than we

do."

'I should've known.' Mandy closed her eyes while they laughed again only for a moment, but it was long enough. The ground rose up and hit her face as soon as she realized she had tripped.

"Ohhh," she moaned, gathering herself up on all fours. It wouldn't be long till the girls dug in on her again. Mandy touched her hand to her face around her mouth and nose then checked her fingers for blood. There wasn't any, but it hurt like there should be some.

She sat up and looked around, but she couldn't see anyone. They were gone. She scrambled to her feet, thinking they weren't far, but there was still no one around. "Claire!"

No answer. Mandy spun round and round in circles, looking in all directions, until she wasn't sure which way they had been headed anymore. "Missy! Erin!"

They couldn't be so far away they couldn't hear her. It was another joke to them. "This isn't funny!"

Mandy's anger was growing. All day they had been picking on her more than usual, but this really took the cake. *'I could've been really hurt.'*

The feeling in her stomach grew too, and she wrapped her arms around her waist. It wasn't hunger this time. It was the feeling she had when something was wrong.

A scream pierced the air, and Mandy tried to look in the direction from where it came. The sound echoed off the trees and bounced all around her. She couldn't be sure which way it came from.

It was followed by laughter. It had the same ricochet effect as the scream which made it more sinister sounding than joking. They needed to quit.

Her heart raced, and she tried taking deep breaths to calm herself. They were trying to get to her, and she couldn't let them see it was working. '*What had Missy said? Keep the sun where? The left.*'

Mandy looked into the tops of the trees until she was dizzy, but there was no sunlight peering through. Without the girls, she was lost.

'*College will be different,*' she told herself. '*New school. New friends. Better friends.*'

She hesitantly took a few steps in the direction she thought they had been headed. She took one deep breath after another while rapidly blinking, trying to hold back her tears. They had gone too far this time. She'd never forgive them for this, but for now, she couldn't let them know their dirty trick worked.

Mandy stopped and looked around again. They couldn't be far. They'd want to watch her panic. There was more giggling, and she pivoted right hoping to catch one of them peeking out around a tree. It was followed by another scream, but it sounded far off ahead of her. The echoing made it difficult, but she went with her gut and followed the noises they were making like it was breadcrumbs.

"Maaaaannnnddddyyyy."

"What was that?" She froze. The whispered voice sounded like it had circled around her head. Her heart thumped hard enough to physically hurt her chest. Then she doubled over from the sensation in her gut. The urge to get sick hit her, but she swallowed it down. Thanks to the way they were always treating her she had nothing to help if she threw up, not even a mint to take the taste out of her mouth.

'I should've stayed home.'

More giggling.

The sound of her friends baiting her moved her feet. Mandy carefully walked on with her head down, muttering under her breath. "I'm going home. As soon as we get somewhere, anywhere."

There was a rustling on her right, and she braced herself. One of them was going to jump out and scare her, but she was ready. *'Go ahead. When I punch you in self-defense because I didn't know what was coming at me, it'll be your own fault.'*

Whoever was making the noise stayed hidden. "That's it. I'll take a bus. I'll call my mom if I have to."

"Mandy! Where are you?" It sounded like Claire, but she wasn't sure. Served them right if they got lost while acting like jerks.

'If they're lost, I'm lost.'

"No." Mandy kept walking. She shook her head trying to knock the thought completely out of her mind. The panic waves and nausea were returning. "Focus." She thought about summer plans like the Grateful Dead tickets she had for their 4th of July concert in New York. Her aunt was taking her, so she wouldn't be putting up with crap like this during it. The distraction of thinking about the concert didn't last long.

The laughter came at her in waves from all directions. She paused and waited. It made it difficult to know which way to go when they played games like this. A couple minutes passed until she heard it, more isolated this time and followed it as best she could. "I'll hitchhike if I have to. Anybody else is better than these three."

"Mandy." It sounded like Erin, but she just didn't know

anymore. "Help me, Mandy."

She shook her head and felt her face redden with anger. There was another scream. It was right next to her like someone's mouth was an inch from her ear. The shriek reverberated off her ear drum, and Mandy covered her ear with her hand in pain.

No one was there.

The tears broke free and fell silently down her cheeks while she worked hard to stop the full sob that was choking her throat. They could go to hell. She would never forgive them for this.

The sun broke through the tree tops, and Mandy finally had visual proof she was heading in the right direction. It was on her left like Missy had said it should be. She looked down and saw her arms were covered in scratches from the various trees and bushes she squeezed through. It was too late to grab a branch now to beat a path to prevent getting hurt. She just kept walking, hoping something would appear soon even if it was one of the girls she currently despised, but she wished for the town of Appleton to be just ahead.

Time dragged on without another noise. There hadn't even been a rabbit scurrying away from her heavy footsteps showing her she wasn't alone. Luckily, the sun's rays were still shining through telling her she was headed the right way.

Then the tree line broke. Mandy walked out of the woods confused and disoriented. This couldn't be right. She'd been walking for hours. At least, it felt like hours. The rumblings from her mid-section were definitely screaming she'd missed a meal.

She blinked several times then rubbed her eyes. It was all

still there. Erin's car was on the side of the road only now there were multiple other vehicles around too. A tow truck was getting ready to lift it.

'How're we going to get home now? Erin's parents are going to be livid.'

There were a couple cop cars and some strange white van behind an ambulance that was angled in the middle of the road as if to block traffic.

'What traffic?'

Two police officers stood near the car, and their mouths gaped open in shock when they noticed her. She walked to the edge of the road, and they continued with their unblinking stares.

'What is all of this?' Mandy scanned from left to right trying to count the vehicles. There was a fire truck much farther down the road in the opposite direction, again parked askew like this road actually saw a lot of cars. Three cop cars, maybe four. The one near the end was hidden except for the rear bumper by the front of the ambulance. *'For a broke down car?' Oh, they must be looking for us.'*

"Miss?"

Mandy heard the officer, but it wasn't registering in her mind he was talking to her. The sun was just starting to fade in the sky, and the lights from all the rescue vehicles were dazzling. She felt like she walked into an alternate dimension.

"Miss, are you alright?" One of the officers asked walking toward her.

"Ye-yes," she said, staring at the vehicles around the ambulance. The feeling in her gut was raging war again. "What's going on?"

"Is this your car?"

"No." She shook her head and finally looked at him. "It belongs to my friend Erin."

The officer nodded and looked over her shoulder. "You and your friends, you went in the woods?"

"We thought it would be quicker to hike to Appleton that way instead of walking the road."

He jotted something down in his notebook.

"We hadn't seen any cars, so we didn't think there'd be much luck staying on the road."

The badge read A. Sanders, and Mandy wondered what his first name was. It was a weird thought to flash through her mind.

"Where are your friends now?"

Her head snapped to look at him. *'My friends.'* She panicked and the world spun around her. Her arms flew out for support, and the officer grabbed her, lowering her to the ground.

"My friends," Mandy began. It suddenly occurred to her she had only said Erin's name, but the officer had been saying friends, plural, the whole time. "I got separated from them. They're in the woods."

"How many were in your group?" he asked.

"Four, counting me."

The officer nodded and continued to scribble in the little notebook he carried.

One of the paramedics rushed over and tended to her. He knelt next to her on the side of the road and checked her pulse and blood pressure while asking a list of questions. "How long have you been in the woods?"

Mandy checked her watch, but it had stopped at 3:30 which was strange because she was positive she wound it that morning. "I'm not sure. A few hours at least," she said.

"What day?" The officer asked.

"What?"

"What day did you go into the woods?"

"Today," she laughed.

The look on the officer's face as he continued to wait for an answer told her he didn't find it funny. *'Great. We were probably trespassing.'*

When she tried to speak again, she could only croak. She cleared her throat, and said, "Monday." There were no signs posted anywhere. None of them better get in trouble for this.

"Monday," the officer repeated. "How long did you say you think you've been in the woods?"

Mandy shrugged and tried to think back. "We were in Appleton a little after noon. What time is it?"

"It's going on seven," the officer answered, "on Friday."

That couldn't be right. There was no way she'd been in the woods five days. Mandy moved to get up, but the paramedic put his arms on her shoulders and held her still. Everything started to spin as soon as she tried to stand, so she didn't object. Her heart raced and her mind went numb. This wasn't right. It couldn't be.

"I need you to sit tight a little longer. We should have you seen at the hospital, run some tests."

"I'm fine." Mandy insisted, but she didn't move. "I just need to find my friends."

"How did you hurt your head?" The paramedic motioned at the side of her face.

"What? I didn't." Mandy was confused.

The officer nodded while studying the area of her face. "That's a rather large gash you have there."

Mandy lifted her hand to her head and touched her temple gently. She winced in pain. It felt soft and gel like, but there was nothing on her fingers when she pulled them away.

"It's an old wound." The paramedic poured a clear liquid onto some gauze and carefully wiped at it. "But it's been seeping still. Looks infected too."

She didn't remember hitting the side of her head when she fell. Her mouth and nose had hurt. For a while after she got back to her feet, her nose ran, and she checked repeatedly for blood thinking the fall broke her nose. It never bled. *'Could it have knocked me out for days? Why didn't they find me? They hadn't been far ahead of me when I fell.'*

"Let's get you to the ambulance. Can you stand?"

Mandy muttered that she could, and the two men each took an arm, helping her to her feet. She looked ahead of her at the trees. Something just wasn't right, and that feeling in her gut was screaming at her to pay attention. She heard them. The voices had been everywhere. *'They were there after I fell. Weren't they?'*

"Is that why you're here?" she asked the officer. "Did my friends send help?"

"Your friends..." The paramedic repeated the words, but glanced at the officer instead of saying more.

"The important thing right now is seeing you get treated," the officer said. "Don't worry about anything else. We've already located your friends."

They kept hold of her while she turned to walk to the back

of the ambulance. Her head pounded now that she knew she was injured. Each step vibrated through her skull like someone had hit her. One of the cars had moved, and she could see the van clearly. A word on the side of it made her stop in her tracks. "Coron-..."

Mandy screamed until sound could no longer emit from her throat. There was a flutter of wings behind her as a flock of frightened birds escaped the trees and took to flight to get away from the noise. She fell to her knees in the middle of the road. On the edge of the shoulder across from where she had been, she saw what was previously hidden by a police car. There were three body shaped forms covered in thick plastic bags.

Chapter Fourteen
Hangman

There was an eeriness to the silence of the lobby as Alice watched the wind blow the snow in circular waves across the far window of the Great Hall. The crackling sound of the fireplace was too far to reach her ears, and the inn was empty save for the family who owned it, the staff, and the ghosts who lived there. Through the window, she watched the winds pick up even more ferociously and was thankful to be inside. Just by watching the snow dance and fly around at the bequest of the winter air, she shuddered with a chill.

It was odd how something this beautiful to look at could be so disruptive. Her shift had ended hours ago. The employee relieving her was late due to the weather forcing Alice to hang around until she arrived, but she never did. By the time she called back saying she couldn't make it in the storm, Alice was already stuck at the inn until the morning if not longer. There was a room available for her to use, but not till she finished pulling a double. The only point of manning the desk on a night like this was to answer calls until the phone lines went down and assist the guest who were trapped by the storm same as her.

When the first shift position opened, she lunged at it. With her seniority, it was hers, hands down. There was less activity during the day. That's not to imply there wasn't any. Ravenwood's secrets were always on the move, but during the day, they were quieter. Alice often thought there was no difference in the energy levels, but the living was in full force around here during the day making it harder to notice whatever lurked in the shadows.

This was the only downside to changing hours. If her relief was late, Alice had to stay until she showed. If she called off, Alice worked both shifts unless someone else was willing and able to pick up the hours. The evening shift was shorter because the desk was covered by the family overnight, and she typically was able to leave when it was over. Today was a double strike against her. None of the part-timers could make it to the inn as well, and Alice couldn't make it home until the plows came.

The snow swirling in relaxing designs outside the window captivated her and almost put her in a trance. Something was coming. It wanted to show itself and needed the energy, her energy to do it. Whenever she felt the most at ease here was when the most activity occurred. It calmed her first to lower her guard. It was how it garnered the biggest reaction, the largest shock value when the ball dropped.

It never revealed itself. Alice never knew from day to day what was terrorizing her, but some days, she had suspicions about what force might be the one at work. The Lady of the Woods and the trees were the usual choices, but tonight she wasn't so sure. That window held its own history, and she felt like it was John beckoning her closer with the twirling snow. It could be all three combining their efforts to reap the rewards when something jumped from the shadows and she finally screamed.

John had worked for the inn for over twenty years. He came here straight out of high school with barely an ability to sign his name. College was out of the question, and the factory jobs in the city were laying off at the time instead of hiring. Like everyone who worked at Ravenwood, he came to the job thinking it would be temporary until something better opened elsewhere.

No one ever left. The trees wielded too much power. It was never mentioned, and it certainly wasn't declared anywhere officially by the owners. There was something in the atmosphere every employee sensed.

Employees were chosen by the trees. That's why the hiring was so random. No other inn had a certified teacher cleaning guest rooms four days a week in the entire country. Judith could get a teaching job anywhere if she wanted like had been her plan when she went to college. Unfortunately, she took a job here while she was still in school, and the trees won't release their hold.

Guests were free to come and go. They kept the inn open and provided a living for the Weaver family. Sometimes, the guests didn't make it out, but it was rare. The victims of the woods were typically trespassers or travelers stranded along 116, not aware of the danger caused merely by their presence.

The family members were stuck. This was their living nightmare. Trips into town by the Weavers for any reason weighed heavily on everyone. The woods loosened its grasp when they were gone because the trees were watching them and awaiting their return. Rumor had it the trees' reach was far and wide. The family couldn't escape no matter where they went. Poor Rosemary's husband was proof enough if anyone wanted to find evidence to back up the claim.

It wasn't much better for the employees, but they were at least allowed to go home, to enjoy vacations. Well, they could take them, but their enjoyment of them was debatable. When they drove down the lane to leave at the end of their shift, the forces residing in Ravenwood pressed on them. It was a thick, heavy blanket of torment which made the desire to leave increase as well as the fear of doing so. Their arrival for the next shift brought a feeling of approval from the woods like they had passed a very important test.

None of it stopped when they were off the property. Anytime someone mentioned a job opening, trying to drag an employee away from the inn, the darkness returned. Seeing a "Now Hiring" sign in a shop window had the same effect. The woods stayed with them wherever they were, and reminded them of the dangers they would face.

John soon learned as everyone did. Once Ravenwood takes you in, there is no leaving it, not unless it's in a coffin. Very few retired from the inn. The ones who did still never strayed far. The woods were in their soul, and the feeling of being trapped never left them. The trees didn't claim the lives of too many employees, but John was one of the unlucky ones. Most of them passed of a heart attack in their sleep or some kind of accident outside of work. Whenever an employee died away from the property, their life was scrutinized by everyone trying to rule out the woods' involvement. To most it sounds crazy, but to the folks in this part of the state, it's a part of life.

Alice was almost to the window before she realized she had left the desk. When she snapped to from the trance she was in, a loud noise behind her made her jump, and she let out a small scream. She slowly turned around with her eyes closed. Her heart beat fast, and she was filled with fear over what she might see when she opened them.

It took her several attempts to have a look. *'Take a deep breath and open your eyes.'*

The breathing was the easy part, but she'd chicken out when it was time to see what, if anything was there. It took four tries, four pep talks followed by four deep inhales before she was able to do it.

It was nothing. A mop left in the great hall by one of the janitorial crew had fallen to the floor. Alice took slow, deep, deliberate breaths to steady herself. Nothing happened by accident here. Something knocked it over, trying to scare her, knowing it would work.

The great hall had been divided up. The far side was used for parties which were extremely rare unless you counted the family events all employees were invited to attend, required to attend. All of the brochures made the claim of elegant enchantment with beautiful pictures depicting a real life fairy tale. Someone had thought the inn would make a great backdrop for weddings and receptions which it definitely had the look to do so, but very few people wanted to spend such a happy day at a place filled to the brim with evil.

At the front of the great hall were a half dozen tables and chairs set up for the guests. It was where the breakfast part of the bed and breakfast was served. Rozalia was there most mornings rambling to guests and staff alike about days gone by. In her youth in Hungary, the most dignified of noble guests would fill the great hall for dinner and dancing. The out of towners were easily amused by her anecdotes considering the woman didn't appear to have cleared her forties yet, but was talking about having lived through the First World War. No one was certain how old she was, but mid-seventies was the best guess.

As Alice made the full three-sixty turn back to the window, her heart stopped. In the seconds that passed since the mop fell, the tables and chairs had been rearranged without a noise. The tables were pushed together, and all the chairs were stacked high atop them like a tower which could easily collapse. She would not be touching them tonight, or any time soon for that matter.

Whoever came to set them back to right, whether it be janitorial or someone from maintenance stuck with the task, would curse her under their breath the whole time. It wasn't Alice who did it, but it was her energy that made it possible. Everyone grew numb to the activity at the inn except for her. Alice would never become immune to it for as long as she lived.

When she faced the window again, she saw him, rather his shadow was present. It was easy to make out the body shaped darkened figure against the glass, and it could only be John. The stories of all the employees who lost their lives on the property were well known. His was the only one to occur near that window.

He started on the janitorial crew and never left his position. He passed on every opportunity to move up whether it was management in his department or switching over to maintenance. Whenever he was asked why, he always replied the same. "With this, I know what I got. Different isn't always better." It seemed like he loved his job, and he did, just not for the right reasons.

John's favorite task was the windows. In the half century plus since the inn had been opened, no one else liked washing the windows. There were too many of them. They were old, odd shaped, and hard to reach regardless of what style of ladder used. And, they were all priceless. The Weaver's made it crystal clear the antiquities in the inn were more valuable than any life passing through it, and that included the inn itself, right down to the windows.

Twice a week, like clockwork, he washed them. It took two days to complete it entirely. One day would be spent on the scaffolding boom outside, and on the next day, he'd make his way through the interior, room by room, except for the family's quarters. They handled most of their own housekeeping. Until he came along, the outside windows were done twice a year if the owners were lucky, but staff signed off as though it was carried out regularly.

It's a wonder the trees never reprimanded those lies. Maybe they did. Maybe those small, seemingly unconnected events like a flat tire or a dog who ran off was the woods form of punishment for a bad shift at work.

Alice wasn't working the night it happened, and she had never been so thankful for anything in her life. The desk clerk was the one who found him. Danni claimed she was looking at the window when she saw him fall and get tangled in the rope. She called for help and ran out the door immediately. It was already too late. The body reeked and was already attracting flies.

Authorities chalked it up to a heart attack. Their version of events was John had died earlier in the day, and his body finally fell off the scaffolding from wind, gravity, or some other unknown reason, got caught in the rope used to prevent accidents in such events, and was long dead before being seen. No autopsy was performed. When it came to Ravenwood, investigations were brief, and the closed cases were never reopened.

Danni told a different story. John was very much alive when his body dropped in front of the window. His eyes were wide with fear, and he struggled at the rope to save himself. No one questioned it. Why would they? Stranger things had happened on these grounds, and that wasn't going to end anytime soon.

It was after his death when the truth seeped out. There were whispers. Gossip was always making its rounds about one person or another. Alice was usually kept in the dark as most of her co-workers despised her existence at the inn, but word of John's exploits had made it to her ears. It only served to illustrate how much talk had been circulating.

When his locker was cleaned out by the owner, she found a camera. Edit Weaver insists she had the film developed as a nice gesture for his family, but even the most gullible person didn't buy that excuse. When the pictures arrived, they set off a new investigation for the police.

The real reason for Edit to stick her nose into John's business was to avoid a lawsuit. His family received the standard the Weavers paid out in the event of an employee death at work which was quite generous for the time. The families of the deceased always filed a lawsuit, but the woods knew where the best dirt could be found.

There was a reason John enjoyed cleaning the windows. The pictures Edit developed were enough for the police to search his home. His wife let them in freely, hoping to clear her husband's name. "It's all a big mistake." She cried while maintaining his innocence right up until the moment an officer removed a large metal toolbox from their shed.

It contained close to a hundred pictures he'd taken over the years of women, some not old enough to be considered women yet, in various states of dress. All taken through the windows he was supposed to be cleaning. It also contained an assortment of women's undergarments they believed he stole from guest rooms while doing his job.

Everyone had a different theory how he was able to pull it off without getting caught for so long. Some thought he used a timer, hanging the camera in front of the windows below where he was currently working and hoped for the best. Others believed he took a risk and hung upside down from the boom. The latter seemed unlikely. If that was how he pulled it off, he would've fallen a long time ago, or been seen by a guest.

The bigger mystery was why the trees waited to act upon it until now. According to what one of the housekeepers overheard a policeman telling Edit, the pictures dated back as far as his first year of employment.

"It's not like they didn't know." Alice said to the shadowy form hanging outside the glass.

Something made the trees act. Alice believed she knew what was in those pictures Edit developed. She was also convinced Edit had an inkling herself which is the real reason she sent the roll off.

Lucinda was growing up, and she was quite the beauty. All the Weaver women had good looks going for them, but Lucinda's looks stood head and shoulders above the rest. There was no limit to what she could've been capable of accomplishing. She could've easily been a model or an actress, but she was destined to a life serving the woods on cursed land.

Alice couldn't have been the only one who caught the way John looked at her. If she noticed, surely someone else did too. Or something else.

John was one of the few who had access to the family's rooms. The Weavers maintained their privacy at all times, and only allowed their most trusted employees inside that wing. When there was a problem they couldn't handle on their own, it was John they called. After Edit's husband disappeared into the woods, with Edit at his side although no one discussed it, she depended on John a lot.

"If he was dumb enough to take pictures of Lucinda, he deserved what he got." Alice shivered and gave the figure in the window one last long look before turning around to head back to the desk. A shadow couldn't hurt her more than her own paranoid thoughts.

The electricity flickered on and off several times, and Alice glanced at the sconces on the wall. She prayed for it to stay on. The generator would kick on automatically, but the great hall wasn't powered by it. The main use for it was in the morning, and the food was prepared in the kitchen. If the power failed, she'd be in virtual darkness save for one small desk lamp.

When it stopped and the risk of outage seemed to be over, she returned her attention to the window. It was no longer a shadow beckoning her. John was hanging from his rope, desperately trying to free himself and spare his life.

The blood curdling scream she emitted echoed off the walls and grew in intensity when everything went dark. Alice fell to the floor in tears. A hundred invisible hands grabbed at her from all directions. It was going to be a long night for everyone at Ravenwood, dead or alive.

Chapter Fifteen
Dead, Presumed Missing

The strap of the bag hung out over the side of the metal trash can next to the dumpster. It was overflowing, and the lopsided lid wouldn't close all the way. From where Ryan stood, all he could see was the strap. He recognized it easily having only handed it over to the owner a few hours ago. The bright yellow with small red lines extending from the sun pictured on the front of the bag stood out.

Seeing it pissed him off for a number of reasons. When he found the bag and what appeared to be an old fashioned reel to reel against a tree near the path through the woods, he got excited. It looked valuable. He thought for sure whoever had lost it, or absent mindedly left it ten feet off the path guests weren't supposed to leave, would be happy enough to have it returned to offer a reward. He figured whoever it belonged to had to still be at Ravenwood or not that far down the road if they checked out because it hadn't been there all morning. When the crew came back from lunch, that's when he noticed it.

"Hey! Look at that!" He called out from the rear of the pack and scrambled over the cheap rope barrier they were replacing. He jogged over to the tree to retrieve it.

The old timers had been yelling at him. "Don't! Come back! Stay on the trail!" They'd been filling his head with ghost stories ever since the project started going on two months ago now, telling him about Ravenwood and the mysteries hidden amongst the trees.

Ryan didn't buy into any of it. He was young, still in his teens and he was sure that's what singled him out as an easy target. They just didn't account on him not being as gullible as they'd hoped. He wasn't going to fall for their stories and wind up the butt of their jokes.

He carried it back and set the reel to reel on the path the crew had finished just last week. The bag looked almost brand new. The back was army green with a yellow strap, and the other side depicted a sunrise over a lake with a wooden toggle button holding the flap in place. He unfastened it, throwing the flap back, and discovered the picture underneath it on the face of the bag was the same.

His boss' voice stopped him after only a brief look inside, but it was enough to see a decent looking camera. "What's all this?" Chuck sounded irritated. He only had two moods: irritated and angry. It could've been worse.

Ryan fastened the flap back on the bag. "Found it over by that tree," he said, nodding off to the side. "A guest must've lost it."

"Guests don't lose anything out this way." It sounded like Tom talking. "The woods take what they want, and they never give anything back."

Putting the strap over his shoulder, Ryan stood up. He lifted the reel to reel and balanced it on his arms. "I was gonna run it back up to the office real quick, so they could find the owner. I'm sure whoever lost it would be happy to have it returned."

Chuck scowled at him. His name was Charles, and he was to be addressed as such. Behind his back, the crew called him Chuck. It took Ryan way too long to understand they called him that not because he hated the name, but because of what it rhymed with. "Make it fast," Chuck barked.

Ryan took off at a sprint toward the inn. He insisted at the front desk to see the owner. He didn't want to simply drop these items off and go. He had hoped to be thanked in some way other than verbally. He didn't really expect the owner of the inn to do much. Coupons for nearby restaurants would've been nice. Most motels had complimentary vouchers from local businesses to hand out to guests hoping to draw in new customers.

The owner of Ravenwood seemed more annoyed than Chuck. She looked at what he had piled on the counter of the reception desk and pursed her lips. "You found this on the trail?" she asked.

Something in the tone of her voice told Ryan to simply answer, "Yes," and not admit to stepping off the path regardless of how close it was.

"We'll put it in the lost and found." She barely glanced his way before disappearing through the office door. If he had blinked in that moment, he would've missed it.

He asked the desk clerk for a piece of paper and jotted down his name and number, asking her to give it to whoever claimed the items.

"What for?" she asked.

Ryan shrugged even though she was staring at the piece

of paper not looking at him. "I don't know. In case they have any questions, I guess." He was too embarrassed to tell her the truth. He hoped they might give him ten or twenty bucks in gratitude considering the camera alone was worth a lot more if he had sold it.

The desk clerk lifted the edge of the flap on the side and shoved the paper into the bag. She set everything under the counter and turned away, dismissing him.

He sulked off and didn't pick up his pace until he was out of the inn. He wasn't out of the rear doors before he regretted not keeping everything. It's what he wished he done now instead of doing the right thing and handing it over to people who probably wouldn't make an attempt to return it. Both options were motivated by money, but one had a more guaranteed outcome.

He sighed and ran toward the trail to catch up with the crew before he was gone long enough for Chuck to dock his pay, but he still debated his choice. *'Where would I have stored it the rest of the afternoon anyway?'*

Now, here it was in front of him again free for the picking, peaking at him from the top of the garbage can. Ryan walked over and knocked the lid off. It fell with a crash onto the edge of the parking lot. The lid rotated slowly as the edges drummed against the concrete in a decreasing crescendo until it finally stopped. He picked up the bag and the reel to reel, carrying them to his car. He felt eyes upon him, sticky and heavy like everyone was watching what he was doing.

'Finders keepers,' he thought. This was the second time he'd found these things today. It didn't occur to him something wanted him to find them.

When he left the property, he was half tempted to head straight to the nearest pawn shop, but it didn't take long before the urge to do the right thing nagged at him. He went home and rifled through the bag, looking for something to identify the girl. There were two notebooks, a camera, a handheld voice recorder, and six mini-cassette tapes for it as well as the reel to reel. The case of each cassette was numbered one through six.

Both notebooks proclaimed "Property of Sue Jennings" on the inside cover. It was a start. One of them was essentially field notes for what he guessed was an amateur paranormal investigation. She had recorded every minute of it, the date and time she set up camp, when and what she ate, every noise she heard, and every attempt she made to contact spirits. It was all there documented in beautiful handwriting down to the most minute detail.

The other was more or less a journal. It was boring by comparison. It mostly included notes about foods she wished she had brought and how uncomfortably she slept the night before. There were a lot of entries about how disappointed she was because her investigation wasn't turning up any proof. Any areas she photographed were noted, and each time she used the handheld in the hopes of catching spirit audio was in there as well except for the last tape.

The most interesting entry in the notebook was one where she called out others in the field. They wouldn't give her a chance because she was inexperienced, but she couldn't get the experience if no one gave her a chance. It didn't matter how many houses she investigated on her own, how much evidence she managed to collect supporting the existence of spirits, they didn't recognize her as an equal. No one would let her accompany them on a major haunting investigation. She had one thing none of them possessed: the guts to investigate Ravenwood.

They all claimed their reasoning for not having come out to this remote neck of the woods was because the owners wouldn't allow it. She thought it was an excuse. They didn't come out here because they were scared. The woods had a vast history of ghostly activity. The tales told about it were taller than Bunyan's blue ox. If any of them had the nerve to come to Ravenwood, they'd be doing exactly as she had done. They'd sneak onto the property from Appleton and set up camp. It's easier to ask forgiveness than permission.

The last entry was dated May 18, 1983. According to what was written, the temperature had dropped quite a bit the previous night, and that night wasn't shaping up to be any different. She hadn't brought enough blankets expecting it to be warmer and was considering gathering enough firewood to create a small fire, risking the smoke giving away her presence. That entry hadn't been signed like the others. Whatever happened that night, whatever Sue decided to do, she didn't come back to the journal again.

The batteries in the handheld had corroded, rendering it useless. The film in the camera would take a week to develop, and the reel to reel was as foreign to him as the subtitled movies his mom liked to watch. There wasn't much more he could do with any of it except track down the woman who lost it. The last entry was close to ten years ago. None of this had been sitting against that tree the whole time which added to the mystery.

He checked the camera. There were only a couple pictures

left on the roll, so he took a random shot of his room then turned it around to face him and snapped what he hoped would be a decent picture. In the morning, he sent it off to be developed.

It would've stopped there. There were many times when he wished it would've ended then. By the end of the week, Sue's belongings that were stashed in his closet had been forgotten. Years might've passed before he stumbled on them again, but then the pictures came in the mail.

The ones taken in the woods were mostly dark making it hard to tell a tree from a shadow. They were uneventful in his mind, but it wouldn't be much longer until the word orb entered into his vocabulary. The pictures were full of them. There was a picture of his messy bedroom then the one where he tried to take a picture of himself. It turned out rather good, impressive, and he would've happily showed it off except he wasn't the only person in the picture. Behind him on the right was a long dark haired woman with her head turned to the side, hiding her face.

Ryan threw the stack of pictures across his room. He wanted everything gone and was tempted to set it to the curb. Remembering how it was put in front of him twice already, he worried it'd find its way back to him, and it was something that just might push him over the edge. He needed to find her, find Sue. He'd give everything back to her, and maybe she could tell him about the woman in the picture. The guys at work had been right. They weren't filling his head with ghost stories. They were warning him.

He yanked the bedding off his mattress and went downstairs. The couch would be his bed tonight. He wasn't sleeping in that room until he found Sue. The strange woman in the picture could have his room to herself.

The next day Ryan went to the city library to search for her, still wanting to return her belongings, but he hoped she could explain the photographs to him. He managed with a lot of assistance from a librarian to go down a rabbit hole in the microfilm reels.

Sue was twenty-seven years old when she went missing out of Ohio. "Missing: Presumed Dead" was one of the articles from later that summer. *'Dead: Presumed Missing was more accurate.'*

Her car had been found on Route 116. It appeared one day on the side of the road rusted and smashed beyond explanation. A picture of the car was included in the article next to a picture of Sue. Someone had their arm around her in the photograph, but whoever it was had been cropped out. It looked like a junkyard had put it in a car crusher only smashing the sides inward until it was almost flat.

It wasn't the car that caught his attention as much. Even more chilling were the trees behind it in the picture. It was the position of the two trees, the way their branches intertwined, and the growth between them spilling out into the ditch. It almost looked like a mouth with its tongue hanging out that had just spewed something up from its bowels.

Ryan walked back home thinking about what he had to do. Her body was still missing. The case had never been solved. As soon as he walked through the door, he picked up the phone and dialed the operator to get a number for the police in Appleton.

It took him about a total of two hours on the phone. He

ended up calling three different numbers, speaking to five different people and leaving two voice mails. Both of which wound up transferring him to a different department when they called back. No one cared.

The last newspaper article he found about Sue said the investigation was still open, but he finally had someone on the phone in Appleton tell him the case was closed. She had died due to an accidental fall into a ravine.

The reel to reel was drug with him to campus when classes resumed in the fall, and he found someone in the audio-visual department who could help him operate it. The kid geeked out over it. A makeshift external power source had been constructed and hooked up to it. It was something that would have been fairly ingenious in 1983. Ryan listened to the nerd noise for as long as he could stomach it, and finally cut the kid off asking, "How do I use it?"

The kid walked him through step by step instructions and began playing the tape. Ryan turned it off. He didn't know what was on the tape, but if it was Sue's last moments, he didn't want anyone else to hear it.

Once he was back in his dorm room, he pushed play. Her voice came across loud and clear. "Sue Jennings, May 18, 1983. It's 6:48 in the evening. I've chosen a place in the ravine to record. Many vehicles and belongings have been discovered in the ravines of Ravenwood."

'Maybe she did fall after all.'

Her voice continued. "I'm going to let this record, and I will check it in the morning."

There were a few noises associated with her walking away, but nothing after that. There was nothing for so long he put it out of his mind and worked on unpacking and organizing his room. Then the humming started.

It was a woman's voice humming what sounded like a lullaby, and he couldn't quite place the tune. The humming became louder or the source inched closer. Either way he almost had the words. It was an old nursery rhyme. Not one of the more popular ones, but his mom was an unending encyclopedia of them when he was little. Then it stopped. There were no other sounds throughout the recording.

Ryan couldn't get it out of his head for days. The mysterious woman on the recording even invaded his dreams. He had to figure out her identity, but was lost as to how. He wondered if there was anything on the mini-cassettes he hadn't been able to listen to, but doubted there was. According to Sue's journals, nothing of note ever occurred.

Not long after that, he was at the store picking up a few things and checking out all the latest gadgets he couldn't afford. He walked right past the handheld recorders for sale. It was a little more than what he should spend.

The curiosity got the better of him, and he grabbed one off the hook, adding it to his basket. He listened to them in order as soon as he got back to his dorm. It was as her notes had said. There was nothing. Then he put the last one in, the one she didn't include in the log. It had even less of nothing which didn't surprise him. The other five contained her voice saying the date and time, asking questions into the woods, requesting spirits to talk to her.

"Sue Jennings, May 16, 1983. It's, uh, 7:34, and pretty dark in this part of the woods. I'm going to attempt contact now."

"Is there anyone with me?"

"Do you have any unfinished business?"

"Why are you trapped here?"

She repeated a lot of the same questions in various areas, but her voice remained the only sound on the tapes. She'd let ample time elapse before moving on to the next one. It didn't surprise him the last one was blank. It had probably never been used. It was dead air.

As soon as he thought those words, he finally heard something. At first, he thought it was footsteps in the woods. Sue had mentioned the weather, so he thought she might've woken up from the cold. The noises grew louder, and he realized it wasn't footsteps. It was a crackling sound. It was a fire. The journals had mentioned she was considering starting one to help keep her warm.

The crackling grew louder and louder. Ryan's skin flushed like he could feel the flames.

"What?" It was Sue's panicked voice.

"No!" She cried out. There was a sound of a zipper followed by Sue again. "Wait... Why is this not... Oh, no!" She was fully panicked.

The zipper could be heard again like someone was running it over the teeth back and forth repeatedly. Then the screaming started.

"Help! Please! Let me out!"

There was a lot of commotion. He couldn't make out all the sounds, but he gathered Sue was trapped in the tent, trying to get free. She had to have a knife, surely she had something like that with her. He faintly heard a voice, her voice, but couldn't make out the words. It sounded like, "Where is it?" That may be his own mind playing tricks on him because he thought she was looking for something to cut through the tent.

More distorted noises followed by the sounds of Sue grunting as she tried to escape. Her voice was muffled, and he realized she had managed to make an opening.

'If she ran from the fire in the dark, she could have easily taken a nasty fall.'

Sue screamed again, and it was followed by a thud then a moan. Ryan was on the edge of his seat waiting for her to escape even though he already knew from the phone calls to the police she hadn't died in a fire. Sue grunted like she was struggling with something. "Let me go!" she screamed.

'Who is she talking to?'

Sue began to cry, and Ryan couldn't understand why she wasn't gone yet. The tears turned into sobs and grew into more screams.

She started coughing. There was a lot of coughing and gagging. Ryan leaned forward closer to the handheld. His heart was racing, and he hoped she'd freed herself. He didn't want to hear what he was beginning to believe he was hearing.

The screams changed. They were high pitched and pierced his soul. She was burning alive. As horrid as it was to hear her shrieks, it was worse when they stopped.

A few minutes later another sound came over the recording. It was hard to hear over the crackling of the fire at first, but it slowly grew louder. More humming, only this time, the mysterious woman sung the tune.

"Here's sulky Sue.
What shall we do?
Turn her face to the wall
Til she comes to."

Chapter Sixteen
Media Frenzy

The call had woke him from a deep sleep. An early riser at the inn had discovered the body at the edge of a garden near the trail entrance and phoned the police. The report on the body sounded strange to his half asleep, barely conscious mind, but given it was Ravenwood, nothing was expected to sound normal. He headed to his office expecting the body to already be in transport to the morgue by the time he arrived. As he drove, he thumbed the steering wheel debating what the cause of death was going to be this time. Bear attacks were getting old. No one ever believed the cover they used regardless of what they went with, but that one needed to rest awhile. Accidental falls were climbing at an alarming speed. "Dehydration," he nodded to himself. If this was the young girl who went missing two years ago, it could be feasible she simply got lost in the woods and died from exposure.

The station was already turning into a zoo by the time he arrived. The woman's family had been demanding answers for years. When their daughter went missing, they discovered the legend behind those woods, and they had threatened from the get they wouldn't take bear attack for an answer. It seems someone had tipped off the local news about the body which appeared out of thin air in the inn's courtyard.

Several officers were manning the doors, keeping the cameras outside. There were two uniforms standing at the front of the swarm trying to keep order. More were needed outside if any other stations showed up, and he had a sinking feeling this was only the tip of the iceberg. One of the officers spotted him and pleaded with his eyes over the heads of the reporters teeming around. He adverted his eyes and walked down the building to a side entrance and swiped his badge to enter. It was too early, and he needed to have the official story straight before he attempted to deal with the buzzards circling around the station with their microphones in hand.

He made his way inside and headed to his office, intending on stopping to talk with the boss on his way. His boss, it turned out, had been impatiently waiting for him to arrive.

"Maxwell!" Chief Cromley's voice carried across the room and caused the higher than normal flurry of activity to pause just long enough to be noticed before resuming.

Cromley had already disappeared before he glanced in that direction, and he picked up the pace knowing better than to force the chief to stick his head out of the door twice. He raised his hand to give the frame a quick knock, but Cromley beat him to it.

"Sit," the chief barked. He didn't look too good like he hadn't slept in days, and he appeared years older than when Maxwell saw him leave the station a little over twelve hours ago. He pressed against his temples with his eyes squeezed shut, and asked, "Did you see the circus?"

"Yeah," he said, sitting down. "They were raising a stink with the officers when I arrived."

"How many?"

"What?" Maxwell wasn't sure which head count the chief wanted.

The chief dropped his hands and leaned into his desk. "How many stations are out there?"

"Six." Maxwell counted in his head. "Maybe seven."

"Crap." The chief grabbed a bottle of pills from a drawer, dumping several into his hand. "That's twice as many from when I arrived not more than twenty minutes ago." He tossed the white tablets in his mouth and slammed his mug of coffee to wash them down. "Local stations?" Cromley didn't wait for an answer.

"And there's going to be more," he said. The chief left with his mug and returned with the pot, setting it on his desk after refilling his cup. He was nodding and chuckling. "She went national. They're on their way."

"She?" Maxwell asked. "Who's on their way?"

"The Jackson girl's mother. We haven't even officially identified the body yet, but someone at that awful evil place called her before making the call to us."

That was surprising to hear. The station had a long history of a good working relationship with the property owners. Something didn't sit right for the inn to tip anyone off.

"Are you sure it was someone at the inn?"

The chief shot him a look telling him not to carry the thought further. Maxwell forced his smile down. Everyone knows, but no one will admit to it. Not discussing it won't change anything.

"We've got to get ahead of this thing." The chief stared off as he spoke. "A team is being put together as we speak."

Maxwell craned his head to the side. With his expanse

knowledge of the property, he figured he was here to advise on the investigation, but it sounded like everything was underway. "What do you need me to do?"

The chief's eyes slowly traveled across the room until they landed on Maxwell's face. His expression was troubling and cause Maxwell's breath to catch. "I need you to lead the investigation."

He jumped forward in his seat. His heart raced. "I don't work in the field anymore."

The chief nodded slowly and drummed the desk with his fingers.

"Not since the accident," Maxwell went on. "It's been a few years since I did anything without a desk." The truth was he hated being confined to an office and would love the clearance to do the work he loved, but not this. It was crazy to send him back out to Ravenwood of all places with as rusty as he was.

"You're all I got. No one else on the force has the experience you do in those woods. Hell, no one else will go near those woods without wetting their pants. I need you on this. You don't have to step off the courtyard. Stay where the poor girl was found, but you're the only one I trust to run point."

Detective Maxwell sighed deeply. An image of his family briefly crossed behind his eyes, and he shook it out of his head. He'd be safe. He always was when it came to that stretch of road. It was the rest of the officers drawing the short sticks and assigned to accompany him who had him worried.

He braced his hands against the edge of the desk and pushed himself back from it. There was no escaping an investigation this time. A team would have to go to Ravenwood, and he was they only one with enough experience, and courage, to lead it.

The reporters at the station were nothing compared to the zoo camped outside the inn by the time he made it there hours later. *'This won't end well,'* he thought, getting out of his car. One of these yahoos will try to make a name for themselves, try to get a scoop and sneak off onto the property. He'd bet dollars to donuts they wouldn't make it back. If the media was this bad now, he didn't want to think what it would be like then.

It didn't take long for him to be spotted. One reporter broke away from the pack with her cameraman then the whole lot of them swarmed as he made his way to the building.

"Is it true? Was the body of Marla Jackson found this morning?" a young woman asked, shoving a microphone in his face.

"I just got here," he said. "I have nothing for you yet."

"It's being said her body just appeared on the property. Does the department suspect foul play?" another asked.

"This isn't the first time someone has gone missing on this property. Are they connected?"

The questions were fired off from overlapping voices as he fought to make his way through the throng. He could see Edit Weaver ahead of him near the entrance to the inn. Her lips were pursed together in her typical irritated expression, but there was a hint of something else in her eyes. Sympathy maybe, but not. Not from a woman as solid as her.

When he reached her, officers stepped in behind him holding the reporters at bay as their questions continued. He prayed they did the right thing and waited for the press conference when the department was ready instead of wandering off on their own to see what they could uncover.

"Detective Maxwell," Edit said when he approached. "I didn't expect to see you here today."

"Not as surprised as I was, ma'am," he replied with a heavy sigh. "Lead the way."

As they walked through the inn to the courtyard, Edit told him what he already knew. "The girl is Marla Jackson. Looks exactly the same as the last time she was seen two years ago. Hard not to recognize her, but I don't know who called her parents."

"You know as well as I do *what* made that call," Detective Maxwell hissed through gritted teeth.

Edit pulled her lips back into a tight line and exhaled loudly through her nose.

"Anything else?" Maxwell asked before headed out the rear doors.

"She had a necklace. It's missing." Edit raised her hands and shook her head. "Shoes and purse are missing too, but the necklace is the main thing. The girl's mom has been calling constantly asking about it. Gold chain with a sapphire pendant. It was given to her as a gift right before she disappeared."

"Expensive?"

Edit's eyes dropped in a rare show of compassion. "Apparently it had belonged to the girl's grandmother."

Maxwell walked into the courtyard alone and headed to the far corner where the scene was blocked off. The coroner was still with the body. The necklace was lost forever if it wasn't with the girl. No one was searching the woods too deeply.

"Maxwell!" The coroner grinned and extended his hand when he saw him. "It's been too long."

The young girl sat upright on a large rock with her hands

in her lap. She appeared very much deceased and lifelike simultaneously. "Not long enough, Johannsen. How's it look?"

The coroner raised an eyebrow. "Well, she appears to be petrified."

"This place has that effect on people," Maxwell remarked, eliciting a hearty laugh from both men. "But I don't think you're talking about fear."

"No. The body is perfectly petrified. In all my years, I've never heard of one found this perfect." Johannsen looked at the girl impressed by what he saw.

"But?"

"But she's only been missing for two years. Do you know how long petrification takes?"

"I'm guessing more than two years."

Johannsen chuckled. "Yeah. A lot more."

Detective Maxwell looked toward the trail entrance then scanned the entire woods at that side of the courtyard. "Time is different here," he mused more to himself.

"You can say that again. Any ideas?"

"Dehydration." He stuck to what he came up with while driving to the station.

The coroner jotted down a note, and said, "Perfect. Well, that's it for me then. Send the body over when you're done. I'm heading out. This place..."

Maxwell nodded. "I get it." He glanced at the body one last time and motioned for it to leave with the coroner. Experience taught him it was a wasted effort in these parts to be thorough. If it wasn't for the family, and the media, they wouldn't be out here en masse like they were.

He gave the officers explicit instructions. Guests weren't to leave the trail, so the search would be confined to a small radius around it unless something was discovered during it. *'Which it wouldn't.'*

"Stay with your partner! Move slowly. Watch your footing. Do. Not. Disturb. The. Trees. If you don't bother them, they won't bother you."

The teams headed out to their assigned grids, and a rippling effect went through the branches of the trees on the edge of the courtyard even though no breeze could be felt. They were afraid, and the trees were showing their appreciation as they absorbed the fear dripping heavy in the air. Maxwell hung his head with his hands on his hips hoping they all made it back out.

It hadn't been ten minutes before shouts came from the trees. Maxwell headed in along the walking trail following the direction they were coming from. He reached the team right as they made their way onto the path. Rodriguez was helping a limping Wilson who grimaced in pain with every step.

"What the hell happened?"

"He fell into the ravine," Rodriguez said.

"I was pushed," Wilson snapped, enunciating his words sharply. "It's broken. I heard the snap."

"For the last time, I didn't touch you!" Rodriguez insisted, letting go of the other officer.

Wilson wobbled a bit as he struggled to stand on his own, and looked Maxwell in the eyes. "I felt a pair of hands on me. I was pushed."

"I believe you," Maxwell said without hesitation. He turned to Rodriguez, and added, "And I believe you too."

The two officers glanced at each other then looked around

at the woods while drawing nearer to one another for protection.

"Help him out of here," Maxwell ordered. He looked into the woods toward the ravine. They got lucky. It was a warning shot, and in his experience, Ravenwood didn't give many of them.

The investigation inside the manor wasn't fairing much better. No one knew anything about the reappearance of the girl's body or the tip to the police. In fact, every staff member claimed they learned about it from other staff or the owner. The guest who phoned it in didn't exist. It seems no one inside the castle was aware of the body in the courtyard until the police showed up.

Those interrogations ended soon after the security footage was reviewed. The girl appeared out of thin air. According to the time stamps on the tapes, there was quite honestly a decorative rock, possibly large enough to be considered a boulder, one second, and the next, the body of poor Marla Jackson was posed atop of it. The tapes were sent off to evidence, but Maxwell knew nothing would come of it. There had been no altering or tampering with the cameras or the footage.

"Time is different here," he told the officer who brought it to his attention. The poor kid hadn't been on the force long and was pale as freshly fallen snow. He couldn't wait to hightail it out of there back to the station.

Not more than thirty minutes after Wilson's *accident*, the investigation was called off. Chief Cromley was still working up a reason to assuage the girls' parents. Both of them aware nothing would be good enough for them to accept.

Maxwell called his men back and watched the relief flood their faces as the fear began to subside the moment they stepped into the gardens of the courtyard. He couldn't breathe easily yet. It was a good thing the investigation was being cut short. The faster they got out of there the better their odds, but he couldn't exhale until everyone was accounted for and safe.

They should've left the moment Wilson was injured. Every minute past that was pushing their luck. The trees weren't happy with them. The officers were invading their personal space, and there were just too many of them for the trees comfort.

He'd been right to be worried. Gorski and Buchanan were still out there, left to the woods in a fight not fair for anyone regardless of how well they could manage otherwise. Nothing could defend you against Ravenwood.

Buchanan had acknowledged when the order to return was given. Whatever happened was recent. Maxwell checked the grid and ordered the teams to search the area for the men. Nobody moved.

"That's an order!" he barked. The looks on their faces fell, and they entered the woods expecting to face their own demise. Maxwell folded and unfolded his arms several times before trying to command his body to fight the nerves.

"Fifteen minutes."

The woman's voice behind him caused him to jump. "What?" He looked around surprised to find Edit Weaver watching a couple feet away.

She nodded toward the last of the officers disappearing into the woods, and repeated herself. "Fifteen minutes." Then she walked back toward the rear entrance of the inn.

Maxwell immediately phoned the chief to update him. "I'm calling them back after ten minutes," he said. Even as the words left his mouth, he realized it wouldn't be that long. He was giving them till the end of the call or five minutes, whichever came first.

He didn't know, more importantly didn't want to know, why Edit put that time frame on the search. She had always been a woman of few words and friendly wasn't an adjective ever used on her. If she came to him with this little tidbit, he was surely going to pay attention.

"What a mess," the chief groaned. "The coroner has agreed to rule it dehydration."

Maxwell was too worried over the fate of the teams in the woods to enjoy being smug over calling it. "What about Gorski and Buchanan?"

"Accident." The chief sighed.

'Not a bear this time?' Maxwell immediately chastised himself internally for the joke. It wasn't the time. He radioed for the officers to return. They didn't need to risk another second in the trees when a cover was already in the works. It was going to be an expensive story too. He didn't want to get caught up in the thought of how much hush money would be paid to their families.

"We'll say one fell in the ravine, and the other fell trying to save him." There was a series of muffled curse words and contained screams on the line. "That Jackson girl's family is responsible for this. They had to turn this into a spectacle."

"It's their daughter," Maxwell said solemnly. There was no length he wouldn't go to for someone he loved.

The chief chuckled, and it sent an unnerving chill through

Maxwell's body. "Yeah, well I just got off the phone with WGGB. Apparently, they've decided to take out a commercial asking the public for help and criticizing our department."

"Has anyone told them they're more than welcome to come search the woods themselves?"

"Only every time I spoke with them. Who knows what they'll do after that forensics lab in Boston gets done with their daughter's body?"

"What lab?"

"They're not happy with our coroner's findings. Seems like they knew enough to have been prepared too. Some lab in Boston wants to study the remains, paying handsomely from what I heard around here."

Maxwell kept his eyes glued to the tree line counting teams as they emerged from a nature version of Russian Roulette for the second time that evening. "That might not be good for us."

"You're telling me."

The so called experts at the lab were just as baffled as they were. Rumor has it the body is still there. It's brought out of storage from time to time to be examined again, but they're more puzzled by it than the locals. The folks in the area were more concerned with the deaths of the officers. Funerals were held. Caskets were lowered into the ground. But did anyone actually see a body? The reach of the trees extends past the badge. It was a first for Ravenwood.

Chapter Seventeen
Moss Farms

The car rolled to a stop along the state road in the middle of nowhere. Tiffany kept her eyes down and her hands clasped firmly in her lap. They should've stopped in Appleton and had the car checked out, but Josh insisted they could make it home. He didn't want to pay an obscene bill at a garage and have to shell out money for another night in a motel. That was his motivation to get back where his buddy could take a look at it. Whether he believed it was a good idea to push their luck with his old beater, or whether he even had the slightest clue what was wrong with it to cause the noises it was making, didn't play a part in his decision at all.

And she knew it.

He hadn't fooled her at all with his talk back at the service station saying it wasn't as bad as it sounds. It was a matter of time before they ended up stranded, but she truly thought the car would make it a little farther than it had. She wasn't sure exactly where they were, but they hadn't passed the turn off for the inn yet which meant they were deep in the heart of Ravenwood. It was the last place she ever wanted to find herself.

Tiffany pulled her phone from her purse and tried to call her dad. All she got was a recording about being unable to reach the cellular subscriber. She looked at the screen, and they were in limbo. There were no bars. It was definitely Ravenwood.

"Who you calling?" Josh asked.

"No one," she sighed, dropping her phone back in her purse. "There's no signal."

He cracked a smile at her. It wasn't a genuine smile. It was the goofy one he got when he thought he was being tricked or when she did something he thought was dumb.

Josh grabbed his phone from the center console and unlocked it. His face fell, and she knew his phone was showing the same thing. There was no service here. He tried to make a call anyway. Then attempted another one and another one followed by sending a few texts. His reaction told her what she already guessed. Nothing went through.

"Where are we?" she asked.

Josh didn't answer her directly. He growled and slammed his hands down on the steering wheel. It was his fourth attempt to start the car again without luck. He popped the hood and cursed under his breath as he got out.

She propped her elbow on the passenger door and rested her head on her hand. Outside the car, he was still uttering a stream of profanity as he kicked the tire, the road and whatever else his feet could find.

Tiffany didn't know much about cars, but as a linguistics major, she understood languages. What Josh was so eloquently saying translated to, "We're screwed! If we survive the night, it'll be a miracle."

Her parents were expecting them. They should be at the house in a couple hours for dinner before going home. When they didn't arrive, they'd try to call. If they couldn't reach her, they would come out to look for her bringing every person they could convince to help be it the police, friends or family, or the National Guard if her dad thought he could convince them to come. They begged her not to drive that route. "Take the long way around. It doesn't matter how late you get in so long as you're safe," her mom had said.

It wasn't entirely up to her, and she made sure her parents knew Josh was planning on taking 116 because it was quicker. "Besides, it's not a crime to drive it. Not even to the trees. So long as you stay on the road, you're fine."

It wasn't that he didn't believe the stories surrounding the old inn. He just never believed it was something that would hit close to home. The people who fell victim to the trees had no one to blame but themselves for whatever they did to cause the woods to claim them. Tiffany never felt it was always so simple.

All they had to do was stay with the car and wait it out. It was already too hot with the air conditioning off, and they'd be miserable before night fall. Even then, the temperature wasn't expected to drop too much, but it'd be a bit more bearable than it was now. By the time her dad showed up, she and Josh would be at each other's throats between the heat and his carelessness causing them to be in this situation, but they'd get through it.

Rather, if Josh started thinking with his logical brain instead of his, 'I'm a man. I have to fix this mess I caused brain.' They would make it.

He walked to the passenger side and opened her door. The heat blasted inside suffocating the last remnants of the air conditioning trapped in the car. "Well, it needs to be towed."

Later, she'd total up the cost of a tow truck versus a night in a motel, but now wasn't the time for that fight. "I figured as much. We'll have to-"

"Oh, you figured it huh? And if you knew what was wrong with the car, why didn't you say something before it broke down?"

Tiffany took a long slow deep breath in through her nose and exhaled through her barely parted lips. They couldn't do this now. She painted a smile on her face, and said, "I figured by your reaction while looking at the engine it wasn't something easily fixed on the side of the road."

"My reaction? How would you know? You stayed in the car. You can't see me through the hood." He pointed to the windshield where the hood was still up blocking her view.

'Why does he always get this attitude when he knows he messed up? He always has to make someone else the bad guy.'

"No, but I could hear you clear enough," she said, not trying to hide her irritation both over his outburst and his interrogation.

The passenger door slammed shut, and Tiffany closed her eyes, taking deep breaths to relax herself. The last week had been tense. She received a job offer over the phone and would be moving in less than ten days to take it, with or without Josh. The apartment she rented was in her name only. He had no job, and the leasing office said the application had better chances of approval without including him. They were there for four full days, and he practically begged for a job at every business in the city whether they were advertising open positions or not. He hadn't heard from any of them yet.

'He's just stressed.' It was making everything worse. Josh normally ran hot, but he was never this bad. Even as she

thought it, Tiffany sadly realized it didn't matter. If this was him under pressure, this would be him from time to time throughout their life together. She didn't really want to deal with it whenever life threw them a curveball. She needed to move to New York alone.

"Let's go!"

Tiffany's eyes flew open, and she looked around to see where Josh was. He was standing in the middle of the road, with his hands raised up in the air, looking even angrier.

"Go where?" she asked. She opened the door and stepped into the hot sun and repeated her question, guessing he couldn't hear her in the car.

"Back to Appleton," he said. His eyes widened, and he looked at her like it was the dumbest thing she'd ever asked. "The car is dead. Our phones don't have service." He looked in both directions down 116. "And you know no one else will be along anytime soon."

"My dad will come."

"You talked to him?"

"No, but I told him you insisted on coming this way. When we don't show up for dinner, he'll look for us."

Josh put his hands on his hips and looked at the road where he was rubbing the pavement with the toe of his shoe. "So it's all my fault."

"Enough!" Tiffany rubbed her eyes with her hands. She was already feeling the heat of the late July afternoon. "Just stop with it, Josh. Nothing is your fault."

'Don't go making this any worse than it already is,' she pleaded quietly.

"It'll take hours before he gets here." Josh sounded calm

finally.

"I'm aware," she agreed.

Josh rubbed at the back of his neck and stared down the road in the direction they came. "We haven't hit Ravenwood yet. We didn't pass the drive. We're safe."

Tiffany had started to nod, but stopped when he finished his thought. Just because they hadn't made it to the inn didn't mean they weren't there.

"If we stick to the road..."

"Josh," she said. This was ridiculous. It was in the top three things everyone around here was taught as a child.

Don't talk to strangers.

Safety in numbers.

Stay in the car if you break down on 116.

"We don't have water, honey. We have nothing. It's hot, and it's going to get worse. We can't be more than five or six miles out. Wouldn't you rather wait for your dad in an air conditioned restaurant?"

'Of course I would! I just don't want to do what I have to do to get there.'

"Fine," she agreed. People had walked 116 without problems. There were some who bragged about it anyway, but she always wondered if they weren't being truthful. "Fine!" She grabbed her purse from the car and joined him on the road.

"No shortcuts," she said sternly. "And I'm not leaving the white line on the far side of the road."

Josh grinned and nodded. "Okay."

Tiffany checked the time on her phone when they started walking. It was 2:54. She'd walk fast which meant it shouldn't take more than an hour and a half to get to Appleton if Josh's estimate was right about how far out they were. Searching her memory, she recited every prayer she could remember learning in Sunday school as a child hoping it'd help.

"There!" Josh yelled excitedly after not even fifteen minutes of walking.

Tiffany's head jerked up and she scanned the area around them, but she only saw the road guarded by trees on one side with an open field on the other. "There what?" she asked. Sweat was beading down her face, but the heat couldn't have got to him that quickly.

"Over by that culvert," he pointed.

"Did you see something?" Her heart skipped a beat, and she turned around. The car was still there. It looked tiny in the distance, but she could still make out its form. They could make it back.

"Look," Josh insisted. "Don't you see it?"

Tiffany didn't want to turn back around. She didn't know what had caught Josh's eye in those trees, but she wasn't brave enough to look. People said there was a witch in the woods, a dark haired lady capable of anything. If she looked you in the eyes, she could make you do her bidding. It was a ghost story told to scare the wits out of children, but in that moment, it was the realest thing she knew in life.

His laughter would've been pleasing to hear after the way this trip had gone, but now it only confirmed to her the raven haired witch had him under his spell. Josh's hands touched her upper arms, and his laughter continued as voice softened. "Babe. Babe? Are you really that terrified? We're almost there. Look."

She shook her head no violently.

"It's Moss Farms."

'No, that place closed years ago. Josh is hallucinating. Seeing a mirage.'

"The sign is right there. We're past Ravenwood if we were ever even in it."

Slowly she peeked one eye open and stole a glance over his shoulder, looking down again quickly. With a deep breath, she gazed with both eyes. There was an old, weather aged sign behind a tree. Stepping out to the side of Josh, she could see it better. The words "Moss Farms" once a vibrant green were faded. Whatever had been written underneath was too indecipherable to make out.

She shook her head. "That means we're close."

"Exactly!" Josh walked toward the other side of the road. "Closer than I thought. We are right outside of town. The old farm is still there or what's left of it. If we cut through, we can come out behind the old service station on the edge of town."

"No."

"What do you mean 'no'?" Josh whirled around to face her and dramatically gestured behind him with both hands. "It's *right* there!"

"No, I'm staying on the road."

"Why?"

"Something's not right. We haven't been walking long enough."

He threw his arms up and circled around before grabbing her hands, talking softly to her. "Tiffy, we're in the clear. We don't have to kick pavement weaving around these curves until we hit the main drag of Appleton." He nodded to the side of the road again. "We can cut through to the edge of town. It's not Ravenwood. It'll be fine. *We'll* be fine."

Tears stung the corners of her eyes. Her feet weren't coming off the road no matter how hard he attempted to convince her. "No," she whispered, trying not to cry.

"You'd rather take the long way then?"

"No, I'd rather wait in the car."

Josh looked down and sighed. He nodded to himself a few times before speaking. "Fine. You do that. I'll get to the service station and find help to come back for you."

She shook her head violently and grabbed his hands tighter. Her tears quietly made two glistening paths down her cheeks. Sobs clung to her throat, and if she tried to speak, they'd escape with an overpowering force.

"I won't be long. Go back to the car and wait." He kissed her on the cheek and walked away, forcing her hands to let go of him.

Tiffany's tears continued to fall as she watched until he disappeared into the trees. In her mind, she could see the layout of it. The place closed when she was little, so she'd only gone a couple times. The memories were still vivid, and it wouldn't take long for him to make it to the old wooden building where vegetables and homemade décor had once been sold. Ravenwood ran them out of business. As the hype of the activity in these parts garnered interest, fewer and fewer people came out to shop. It was located too close for comfort to the land cursed for all time.

Once Josh was out of sight, she walked back to the car. Tears still flowed freely, and she felt weak and shaky. If she had the courage to walk the other side of 116, they might've seen the bottom of the sign blocked by the overgrowth from years of neglect. The words at the bottom weren't too clear, but they could've made out, "5 mil s ah d."

Back at the car, she sunk on the ground next to it, trying to absorb what little shade there was. It was too hot to be outside long, and she hoped Josh was right. If he was, it probably wouldn't take more than thirty minutes before a vehicle pulled up to help. It was 3:41, and she counted off the seconds while she waited.

Time dragged on and pulled what felt like hotter temperatures with it. She grew tired and worried how much was from stress and how much was the heat getting to her. The shadow on the ground continued to spread until she could lay down comfortably in the grass along the road. It was a little after five, but she wasn't giving up hope yet.

She saw the sign too. As tattered as it was, it clearly read, "Moss Farms." Josh didn't walk into Ravenwood, and it was very likely she wasn't waiting near there either. He was probably sitting in some air conditioned garage waiting for a truck to come back from a call or for an employee to be free to come out for her and the car. He couldn't reach her if he did try to call. Any minute now, she'd hear the grumble of an engine down the road groaning louder as it closed the distance to her.

Tiffany was startled awake. She thought she heard Josh's voice calling her name. There was still enough light to see by, but it was getting dark. She sat up, but didn't see a vehicle other than his. She rubbed her eyes and stretched then slowly pulled herself off the ground. The grass had been more comfortable for sitting, but it left her stiff and sore from her nap.

7:37

Suddenly, she felt very cold, and a shiver tore down her

spine. She leaned against the trunk looking down the road in both directions, but it was empty.

'I know I heard him.'

"Josh!" She called out, hoping he was nearby. Maybe he was walking back to wait for help with her. She squinted down the road toward where he cut through the old farm. The trees were casting longer shadows, and she couldn't see anything in the darkness they had created.

"Josh!"

It must've been a dream. *'But where is he?'*

7:39

Then, she heard it. There was a faint rumble, and she recognized it as an engine. A vehicle was coming. She strained to see as far as she could down 116 toward Appleton, but eventually, the road curved back in a cover of foliage preventing her from seeing too far. The noise grew louder as it approached, but something wasn't right.

Tiffany looked the opposite way and saw headlights coming from the direction of Ravenwood. The truck became larger as it neared, and she recognized it. Her dad had come just like she said he would. He pulled off near the car and jumped out, half running up to her and gave her a tight squeeze.

7:42

"Your mother and I have been so worried. We couldn't reach you by phone, and when I lost signal a couple miles back, I prayed that was the only reason why."

"I know," she said quietly. The water works in her eyes weren't done leaking yet.

"Where's Josh?" he asked.

Tiffany thumbed the air over her shoulder. "He went to get help."

Her dad looked around. "Huh. Well, I can't say as I blame him. I probably would've hiked to Appleton too instead of going to Ravenwood."

"Tiffany!" Josh's voice called out again.

She looked at her dad terrified. Josh sounded like he was injured. Her dad didn't seem to be phased by the pain in Josh's voice.

Her dad smiled. "I meant the inn, of course."

"Did you hear that?" she asked.

"Hear what?" He looked the tree line over. "I don't hear anything."

'It must be the heat playing tricks on me.'

"Come on," he said. "We'll drive into Appleton. Maybe we'll pick him up on the way, but if not, we'll be able to call him to see where he's at. And your mom too. She's probably beside herself now that she can't reach me."

"Uh." Tiffany looked down then glance toward where they had parted in the road.

"He did stick to the road, didn't he?" Her dad's voice sounded concerned and angry at the same time.

She shook her head. "He cut through Moss Farms."

That relaxed her dad a little bit. "You walked that far?"

"It's right down there," she said pointing.

He inhaled deeply and scratched the back of his neck. "Josh went into the woods?"

"Yeah."

"Not far from here?"

She thought about it for a minute. "I could still see the car, but barely."

"Tiffany!" The high pitched agonizing scream pierced the air.

Her dad put an arm around her shoulders and led her to the truck ignoring Josh's screams once again. "Let's go home."

"Home?" Her heart raced, and her breathing became shallow. "What about Appleton?"

He opened the passenger door for her, and she climbed up in the cab. "Josh isn't in Appleton, honey. He's in Ravenwood."

Her dad closed the door before she could say anything else. When he got behind the wheel, she insisted, "No. There was a sign. It said Moss Farms. I saw it!"

He put the truck into reverse and backed away from Josh's car before putting it in drive. "I don't know what sign you saw, but you're closer to the inn. It's a few miles behind you. The old Moss Farms has to be a good five or six miles down the road."

Tiffany panicked. She rolled down her window for fresh air even welcoming the hot blast that hit the cold interior. *'No, that's not right. He can't be in those woods.'*

7:47

Her dad made a U-turn in the middle of 116 to head home, and as he did, Tiffany heard Josh's voice for the last time.

"Tiffany, please! Don't leave me!"

Chapter Eighteen
Housekeeping

He never amounted to much in life and was useless even in death.

There had been a few boys lined up for her back in the day which was a difficult feat given the family name. By the late forties when boys were starting to take notice of her, rumors about her family's property were already spinning off fast tongues. It wasn't all tales about unruly trees and what lurks in the shadows. There were warnings about what a future at the inn held. Any man who married a Weaver woman would always be married to one as she would refuse to change her name. It was the Lady's doing.

It never sat well with Wilbur, and he'd always act shocked when somehow it was pointed out his wife wasn't Mrs. Plummer. She never cared what he called her. If it made him feel better fictionalizing her last name was the same as his, it didn't hurt nothing. It didn't change the fact all the payroll checks were signed 'Rosemary Weaver.'

There was no leaving the inn neither. Small trips if one had the notion were one thing, but the inn was life. The happy couple would work the inn until the daughter inherited, and the business would remain in her name. All decisions ultimately rested on her shoulders. The husband's input was humored, but certainly not necessary.

'But I like him, mama.' The memory of those words echoed inside the car, haunting her for a lifetime based on one severely bad decision.

Other suitors were far better equipped for this life. One had a good business sense about him and would've been beneficial in matters such as cutting costs and drawing in new customers. Another had the work ethic of a mule. He was always working on one project or another and had his own construction business now. Those handyman skills could've been put to good use at Ravenwood.

Yanyo Rose didn't have much to say about it. Maybe if her grandmother would've weighed an opinion, she might've listened. When her mama objected and simply tried to convince her to wait a little while before making a decision, she had answered, "But I *like* him."

A few moments of flirting with attraction traded for two decades married to Wilbur. All in all, he was a pretty decent guy, and he certainly loved her. He just wasn't good for much else besides company.

The headlights passed over a sign indicating there was only ten miles left. It wouldn't be long now until she had answers. That's not the real reason she went to Wilmington. She pretty much figured out what happened to Wilbur already, but she had to see for herself. It was the only closure she'd ever receive.

The closer she got to the motel the angrier she became. She had been afraid when he decided to leave Ravenwood. He thought he could pull a fast one claiming he was going to Florida to open another inn. "We're going to be a chain! Isn't it exciting?"

Rosemary had warned him. Begged him not to go. The woods were capable of more than he gave them credit, and she tried everything she could to talk him out of it.

He insisted it was the real deal. He had ads from Florida papers, listings of properties on the market. Many of them were priced to sell. He had his own money to put into it, an inheritance from his father. Once he purchased it and spruced the place up, he'd open it under the name Ravenwood. "It'll be the first of many."

It was an act. If his own wife didn't believe his story, he shouldn't expect the Lady would be any different. Wilbur never cared for the cold and had always wanted to go back to Florida. His folks moved to Boston when he was in high school, and he met Rosemary not long after he graduated. She'd been honest from the get about where her future lied, but he spent the next nineteen years of marriage trying to convince her to pack up and go.

"I can't," she told him more times than she could remember. "My life is connected to these woods."

When he drove down the lane of Ravenwood leaving his wife and seventeen year old daughter in the rearview mirror, she prayed he'd fall ill like what happened to her grandpa all those years before she was born. If Wilbur became sick, it'd be easy for her to swoop in and bring him back to heal. That's not how it happened. Instead, he was plagued with car trouble from shortly after he left the inn until he reached North Carolina.

He'd spent weeks hanging around small towns, staying in local motels, waiting on another mechanic to diagnose what was wrong with the car this time. Thousands of dollars they'd lost, and he wasn't halfway there yet. "It's my money, Rosey," he told her. "Don't worry about it."

The fear was settling in, and she could hear it each time they spoke. It just didn't have the intended effect. Instead of realizing his folly and coming home, it made him want to reach his destination faster. As if anything in Florida could save him from the reach of these trees.

Then on Monday, no more than a couple hours after leaving the northern part of North Carolina, he called to say he was in Wilmington. He'd been hit with a severe stomach bug and had to get off the road. "Food poisoning," he declared. "I thought there was something off about those eggs I had at the diner this morning."

"Maybe it's time you come home," she suggested.

"I'll be alright," he said, sounding like he was trying to convince himself. "I just need a little rest. I'll be right as rain in the morning."

Rosemary hung up believing he'd call the next day, feeling ten times worse. If she couldn't convince him to head back or if he was too ill, she'd fetch him herself.

The next morning came and went without a word from Wilbur. She rang the phone of his room several times in a row, but there was no answer. It was the first motel he stayed at with a direct line in the room, and she still couldn't get ahold of him easily. The desk clerk sent someone to knock on his door, or he just said he was to appease her after minutes of begging and practically crying. No one came to the door, and he said Wilbur hadn't checked out yet.

Rosemary didn't hesitate. Barely twenty minutes passed from the moment her eyes opened until she was turning out on 116 to bring him home. There had been a bag packed, waiting on the bench at the food of the bed for almost a week. Once the car troubles began, she prepared for this. Wilbur was probably lying in bed feeling near death from whatever illness the trees sent after him. She drove straight there, only stopping for gas. Whenever she pulled off the road, she would drop a dime in a payphone and try again.

The drive took forever, and she was beside herself with worry by the time she pulled into the lot of the small roadside inn. Wilbur's Continental was parked by the street. She'd recognize it anywhere. It was his prized possession. He spent more time with his car than he did his own daughter.

'*It's a good sign.*' She told herself. '*If the car is here, so is Wilbur.*'

She tried the room first. He was in room number eight. After several knocks placing her mouth as close as she could to the frame to yell his name, she gave up and went to the small office, hoping they'd unlock the door for her. Not only was he unable to answer, but she didn't hear any noises coming through the door. His illness overtook him quick.

The employee working the desk was happy to see her and highly irritated with her husband. He had pounded on the office door in the middle of the night, waking the owner and his wife. He screamed at the top of his lungs, rambling about a lady in his room, and the words came out so fast it was hard to decipher what he was saying. After carrying on like a madman for several minutes, he ran back out of the office to his room. The owner came after him, angry and intent on throwing him out, but didn't bring the master key with him.

'*If the lady is here, there isn't much time.*' Her grandfather had longer. His illness worsened, but he was given time to leave Boston even if it was against his will. Wilbur should've heeded the multiple warnings of car trouble the woods sent him.

"By then, he decided it could wait till morning," the clerk continued. "Except your husband was gone when he let himself in the room a little after seven."

"Gone?" Rosemary asked. He wouldn't have left his precious car behind.

"Yeah, the room was empty."

Rosemary looked out the window at the Continental. *'Maybe he's laying down in the backseat.'*

Noticing her gaze, the clerk said, "Good thing you came when you did. The owner was giving him till the end of the week to come after the car before he had it towed."

"What?" Rosemary had been lost in thought and hadn't been listening.

The clerk gave her a condescending look, and added, "I think he's being more than fair. Your husband was quite a nuisance."

"Yes, you're right." Rosemary glanced at the car again. He had to be close by. "Can I get a room please?"

"A room?"

She wasn't sure if the clerk looked more surprised or annoyed. "Yes, I won't be driving back to Massachusetts tonight. Room eight if it's free."

"You want the same room?" The clerk's words came out slowly, and he raised an eyebrow, untrusting about what she, probably what her and Wilbur, were up to.

"My husband is sick."

The clerk scoffed, and she didn't like the meaning he

apparently attached to the word.

"If he comes back, he'll go to his room."

The clerk wasn't convinced, but he wasn't about to turn away a customer either. He slid the book over for her to sign in and got the key. "And what if he doesn't come back?"

It was a simple question, but it echoed through her like an omen. She shivered and batted away the tears in her eyes, swallowing hard. "I'll find him," she said softly, staring at her wringing hands.

The car was empty. No Wilbur. None of his luggage either. Once Ravenwood has you in its grasp, there is no escaping. There's nowhere to flee that is safe. If the lady did take him last night, what's left of him should be here.

There wasn't a trace of him in the room either. It had already been cleaned and made up for the next guest. If any of his belongings had been left behind, the clerk hadn't mentioned it.

The room was heavy with the essence of Ravenwood. It was a gloom hard to comprehend until its felt. Those woods are laced with spirits and fear. It drips off the trees like sap. It's just as sticky, but never turns into anything sweet. She'd been here alright. If Rosemary didn't leave soon, she'd be back for her as well which meant she may have to leave Wilbur as a missing person if he didn't turn up right away.

Rosemary checked in with the staff, but there were no messages for her. It made her breathe a sigh of relief because no news was good news at this point. The lady had come for him, and he ran. She just needed to find him before the lady finished him off. Surely, a man carrying two suitcases and a duffle would be noticed wandering down the highway.

'Unless he left his belongings.' The clerk hadn't mentioned it. There shouldn't have been anything too valuable to steal. It didn't seem likely there was a huge market for men's second-hand middle-aged clothing.

"I'll check into it tomorrow. I'll ask when I leave if he left anything," she said to the room. The list of things she needed to do before she left town kept growing longer. He had an outburst in the middle of the night which meant the lady of the woods had been playing with his mind. If he had a breakdown, he could be anywhere, doing anything. The police station and hospital would be her first calls.

She drifted off to sleep feeling he was close. Things would look better in the morning. She would find him.

When she awoke the next day, her stomach churned and heaved. The lady hadn't given her long at all. *'Or it's from worry.'* It could go either way really.

All of the calls had been placed, but there was no sign of Wilbur's whereabouts anywhere. She had to remain calm and stay positive. Losing it now wouldn't help either of them. It was time to head back to Massachusetts, and she arranged to have the car driven back. Two employees were leaving tomorrow to come pick it up. She'd let the person at the desk know when she checked out not to have it towed, and she'd pay any ridiculous fees if they required it to leave the car a couple more days.

Rosemary sighed and shut the door behind her. "More expense." She threw her suitcase in the backseat of her car. "More time wasted down here tempting my own fate."

She walked into the office to return the key, and the owner came out to talk to her. Nothing had been left in the room, and the car would be fine to stay a little bit longer. The conversation went a lot smoother than she had imagined.

Rosemary pulled out of the lot and headed out of town with a feeling of trepidation pressing on her shoulders. She felt like she was leaving Wilbur behind and had to fight the urge to turn the car around and go back. "He's not there," she said, gripping the steering wheel tighter.

By the time she reached Virginia, her stomach had straightened itself out. It had to be the lady because her worry over her husband had only increased. She couldn't stay there to search for him, but it didn't stop her from sending someone else to do it. She would pay all their expenses and maybe a few other incentives to anyone willing to travel out of state for a few days or however long it took.

Every plan she concocted; every new idea had to be shaken from her mind. "He's probably already come to his senses. There'll be messages waiting when I return." She spent the entire day on the road attempting to convince herself in vain her husband would be alright. When she squeezed her eyes shut to rid herself of the negative thoughts, the lady's beautifully evil face flashed behind her eyelids.

'She's never attacked off the property,' Rosemary reminded herself. *'Only warned.'*

It was late when Rosemary turned off 116 onto the lane to the inn. She was exhausted and had wanted to stop hours ago but didn't want to anger the woods any more than she already had. Unexpected trips were not permitted. She had broken their rules and would spend a great deal of time paying for it.

She pulled along the side of the inn where employees parked and drove to the back where the reserved spots for family were located. They were the only ones allowed to use the far side entrance giving them one of the few shreds of privacy they were allowed. The moment she spotted Wilbur's Continental parked in his spot she lost it and could barely park her own car. It wasn't impossible. Wilbur drove much faster than she did, but it was unlikely she had just missed him at the motel.

The doors were unlocked, and the luggage was piled on the seat when she looked inside. She walked through the inn trying to keep it together. "Any news?" she asked at the desk.

"No, ma'am," the clerk said unable to look at her directly. "I'm sorry."

'He could've gone straight to our wing.' It was the thought she clung to as she climbed the stairs. *'He was tired from the drive just like me and figured he'd bring everything in after a good night's sleep.'*

Rosemary checked on Edit first. She was sound asleep in her bed. The poor girl had been through a lot just from her dad moving away, and Rosemary hoped she wouldn't have to break her heart even more if her dad never reappeared. The hallway loomed in front of her, and it seemed to stretch out farther away as she looked down it toward her room. *'If he's not there...'*

With a deep breath, she forced her body to move, one step at a time. When she reached her bedroom, she turned the knob. It was locked. She pulled out her key and let herself inside. It was empty. There was no Wilbur and no sign he'd been there since she left.

'So that's it then?' She threw herself across the bed and sobbed until sleep finally overtook her.

She thought she'd always wonder how he met his end, but she surprisingly didn't think about it much. The truth would probably be more than she could stand. There hadn't been a single penny in any of his stuff, and his wallet was missing. Judging by the stack of receipts in the glove compartment, Wilbur had blown through most of his inheritance, sometimes changing motels several times a night before settling on one. The lady had her claws gripped into him longer than Rosemary originally thought.

It helped the woods brought his things back to her. She pictured the car traveling the roadway without a driver. It was the only thing capable of making her smile since his disappearance. There'd be a number of legends born from the sightings.

There was typically a five year wait before she could have him declared dead, but she was certain it could be done after one year. His car was here which made it appear he had returned home. Ravenwood's reputation would come in handy for that if nothing else. The life insurance would be helpful for Edit's schooling and much needed repairs to the inn.

Rosemary would've happily waited the full five years if it meant not receiving that call from the Wilmington police department a little over two months after Wilbur went missing. The temperature in her office felt like it dropped twenty degrees as she practically went into shock listening to the policeman on the other end of the line.

"Numerous reports of a smell…"

Surely, it was some kind of mistake. It couldn't be her husband.

"Many attempts to clean and air out the room…"

Not after this long. It would've been located before now.

"The body was discovered…"

Medical records confirmed what she feared. The body found underneath the twin bed in room eight belonged to her husband. It was in a state of decay rendering him unrecognizable. The cause of death was choking.

"Employees stated he was acting in a bizarre fashion. Some sort of mental break is believed..."

Wilbur had choked to death on tree bark, but that's not the only unusual part of his death. The bark was round leafed birch. It was a tree so rare it's thought to be extinct, but Rosemary was familiar with one such tree which thrived in a clearing not far from where she sat listening to the policeman finish his report to her.

"It appears he's been in the room since his death."

Rosemary dropped the phone, and the echo of it hitting her desk sounded much farther away when it reached her ears. *'That's why he felt so close. I was sleeping on top of him.'*

Chapter Nineteen
Car Trouble

Alice watched the leaves blow across the parking lot. This used to be her favorite time of the year. She loved watching the trees turn brilliant colors before the ground was covered in bright reds, yellows and a smattering of purple. Jumping in a pile of leaves had been something she looked forward to as a child. From the first day of school each year, she'd look forward to the day her and her brother would be given the chore of raking. She'd rake her section happily just for the opportunity to spend an afternoon playing in them before her father would come home from work and burn them.

They didn't hold the same joy anymore. It wasn't because she was an adult. She'd still jump in a pile if given an opportunity, but the apartment building she lived in didn't have a yard. Even if it did, she's not sure how the owner would feel if she came along destroying the hard work done to rake it.

No, it was because now the leaves held her hostage. She'd been sitting in her car for thirty-five minutes hoping the winds would die down. Even then, she wouldn't know what to do. If she backed out, she would surely crunch some under her tires.

Everyone said it was okay. They came and went from the property without a second thought to the dead leaves they pulverized with their vehicles. Alice didn't want to risk it. The wrath of the trees was fickle at best. One person could be mutilated over a discarded can while another could urinate off the path without repercussion.

With a sigh, she opened her car door and watched where she placed her feet when she stepped out. There was always a bag packed in the backseat for a variety of reasons. Even when there was no threat of weather blocking her from leaving the countryside inn, there was always a chance of a call off forcing you to work a double.

Alice grabbed her suitcase and went back inside, stopping off at the reception desk to get the key for the room used by employees when there was a reason forcing them to stay. She claimed that her car wouldn't start for the third time this month. Five dollars would be deducted from her next check. When it was almost any other reason causing her to stay the night, the owner didn't charge for it, but her car broke down more often than it seemed to run right. Edit Weaver decided to tack on a fee to help cover the costs of overhead and cleaning when she had to use the room for her own reasons.

'It's worth it. Five dollars is money well spent if you're saving your own neck.'

She entered the drab room and looked around. The entire inn had been remodeled except for this room. Mrs. Weaver had claimed it would be done too, but the remodel ended in the spring. The room reserved for emergencies looked just as worn and gloomy as ever. It was rare, but there were occasions when this room had been lent to actual paying customers. That didn't seem to be enough for the owner to spend the money to have it updated.

The television was old and barely worked. She still

switched it on and turned the volume up loud. The cracking and hissing of the static was better than any noises she might hear with it off. There was no phone in this room which was fine for employees. It would be a very long and boring night. Alice didn't even have a book with her to read.

She grabbed her night clothes from her bag and went to the bathroom to soak in the tub. She showered first then filled the tub as hot as she could tolerate it. After the water went cold, she drained half of it out and added more hot water to it. There was really nothing else to do until she went to bed. She'd stay in the tub until her entire body shriveled up with wrinkles to match her fingers and toes if she could.

The noise from outside the bathroom door stopped. Someone had turned the television off.

'Or something.' A chill ran down her spine at the thought. This room was too far from guest rooms for there to have been a complaint. The only person close enough to hear it would be Caroline, the second shift desk clerk. She'd admitted to Alice that she turned the volume up loud for the same reason, so it wouldn't make sense for her to come in to switch it off.

'Unless there were guests in the great hall.' There weren't any parties scheduled for tonight. Parties were rarely scheduled here. Couples and families did use the tables in the breakfast area to hang out, play cards and whatever else they could think of to kill time. It was possible they could hear the noises and grumbled about it.

Something crashed in the other part of the room. It wasn't loud enough to be the television falling over. It could've been a lamp, but it didn't quite sound like that either.

Alice seriously debated about staying in the bathtub and

ignoring it. The only reason she got out of the water was because if whatever was on the other side of the door came in here with her, there'd be no where for her to go.

She released the plug in the drain and stood up, reaching for where she set a towel at the edge of the sink. It was gone. She stepped out of the tub with water dripping off her body making a puddle on the floor and walked to the rack, but it was empty. There had been two full sets of towels when she entered the bathroom, but all that was left was the washcloth she used in the shower.

'*Keep it together,*' she told herself. It bothered her to think anything had come in the room while she was bathing, human or otherwise.

The only thing she could do was use her nightgown to dry off and wrap it around her body. Once she got dressed, she'd head to the laundry room and dry it. She stepped out of the bathroom and wanted to run.

The mattresses had been flipped off the bed frame. All of the bedding lay in a heap on the floor. Her lower lip quivered, and she tried not to cry. There was nothing she could do. She couldn't risk being seen by a guest with only a wet nightgown wrapped around her body, and her suitcase was somewhere in the mess on the floor.

It took several long minutes before she could move. As quickly as she could, she pushed the mattresses back on the bed and threw the blankets and sheets on top, shaking each of them out as she did. The suitcase wasn't there. Her whole body shook thinking about looking underneath the bed. Alice walked across the room before slowly lowering herself to the floor. It was clear. There was no bag and nothing poised to scare or grab her either.

'Why is it always me?'

No one else at Ravenwood was tortured every day like she was. Some employees went months without a single tale to tell at the end of their shift. Alice was lucky to clock out with only one nightmare to recover from that day.

She grabbed the blanket and wrapped it around her. It still looked bad, but at least she was covered. She went down the side hall and entered the staff area from the back. In the laundry room, she shimmied the nightgown from under the blanket and tossed it into an empty dryer. The material was thin, and she hoped it wouldn't take long to dry. There was minimal staff this time of day which helped ease her mind, but she didn't want anyone to see her.

Alice headed toward the door to the reception desk, planning on opening it a crack to talk to Caroline. As she passed Mrs. Weaver's desk, she had a better idea. She picked up the handset on the phone and called her instead. The trouble she'd be in for walking around the inn wearing nothing but a blanket far exceeded what would be said about her using Mrs. Weaver's phone.

"Thank you for choosing Ravenwood! I would love to help you plan your stay."

It was the standard greeting they were forced to recite. "It's Alice."

"Alice? What's going on? I thought you were staying."

"I am. Have you seen my clothes? Or my suitcase?"

There was a pause on the other end of the line. "No," Caroline finally said. "I'm not seeing anything up here. Are you sure you left it at the desk?"

"It was taken from the room."

"The room? Where are you?" Caroline finally remembered the room didn't have a phone.

"I'm in the office. Don't come in here! I'm only wrapped in a blanket."

Silence again.

Alice squeezed her eyes shut. This was humiliating. "Everything was gone when I got out of the tub, including the towels."

"Ah, geez. Maintenance was saying activity has been high lately. I'm sorry."

"It's not your fault," Alice told her. "Just keep an eye out please? I had to use my nightgown to dry off, so it's in the laundry room. Unless my clothes turn up, that's all I got."

"Yeah, of course I will."

"Thanks." Alice hung up and snuck back toward her room.

The first thing she did was remake the bed to kill time. She often had to fill in for housekeepers when they were short staffed, so she knew how to do it properly. She sat on the chair across the room while tears slowly rolled down her cheeks. Every few seconds, she glanced at her watch, praying time would move faster. She was supposed to work in the morning and didn't have a uniform to wear. There were plenty available, but Mrs. Weaver wasn't going to let her borrow one. It would be hers to keep, and the cost would be deducted from her check along with a charge for the room.

She'd have to go home before her shift in the morning. Once her nightgown was dry, she'd check to see if the wind calmed down. The tears increased and came down in torrents. The lot would still be covered with them, and she couldn't clear the lot and the lane of leaves while wearing her night clothes.

Everyone else came and went without a second thought. *'It didn't matter if it was already on the ground. Just don't harm what's still on the trees.'* Her brother had told her that a hundred times, but she was scared to tempt the woods.

Outside the window, she heard the howl as the wind picked up. It wasn't the wind making the noise. It was the trees warning her. They were reminding her she was trapped. Her ability to leave the property was up to them.

'I'll get another uniform then,' she sighed. Pretty soon, she'd lose her apartment at the rate she kept owing money to Ravenwood.

It'd been twenty minutes since she returned to the room, and she didn't expect her nightgown to be dry yet. She wanted to give it a full thirty minutes, but she felt awkward and uncomfortable. Even though no one was around to see her, it didn't feel right being wrapped in nothing but a blanket.

She turned the television back on, but kept the volume low. *'That's probably why they messed with me in the first place. I was trying to shut them out.'*

Nothing came in clear but an old sitcom rerun. Alice never watched much television, but this show was one she had loved. It was an episode she'd seen at least half a dozen times, but it might keep her distracted while she waited. Anything was better than the silence of the room and the sound of the trees yelling at her along the wind.

The episode ended, and Alice realized she had lost track of time. It'd been over forty minutes now. Her nightgown had to be dry. She made her way across the room to sneak out again, pressing her luck in the hopes she wouldn't be spotted.

The only staff left were Caroline and two maintenance men. If anyone had to see her in this predicament, she hoped it wasn't either of the guys.

There was a quiet knock at the door. Alice jumped back and almost fell to the floor.

"Alice?" It was Caroline.

She gathered the blanket around her again adjusting where it had slipped out of place and cracked the door. Caroline was holding her suitcase in her hands.

"You found it!" Alice threw the door open and used her one free hand to grab it. "Thank you so much!"

"I wouldn't say I found it," Caroline looked at her sharply.

As much as she didn't want to know, the words came out of her mouth anyway. "What do you mean?"

"It wasn't there one second. Then when I got off the phone and turned around, there it was."

"Like someone dropped it off?"

Caroline crossed her arms and rubbed her shoulders, glancing down the hall in one direction then the other. "But who?"

Alice nodded and bit her lip. This wasn't the first time the inn had messed with her, and there wasn't a chance it'd be the last either. "Thank you," she whispered, closing the door.

"Wait!" Caroline grabbed the edge of the door before Alice could shut it and held it open. "The phone call was for you. Bobby needs you to call him right away. He left his number."

Caroline let go of the door and headed down the hall. Alice watched until she rounded the corner in the direction of the great hall back to the front desk.

'Wonder what he wants?' She took the entire suitcase into the bathroom with her to change. Nothing was going to be left out of her sight again after this. *'Where is he that he had to leave his number? Mom and dad's number hasn't changed.'*

Alice got dressed and threw the blanket on the bed. She took two steps away then stopped. It bothered her how disheveled the room looked. Bobby could wait. She finished making the bed before going to the desk to use the phone.

She stared at the piece of paper Caroline handed to her. It had been months since dad came home from the hospital after his heart attack, but she had called the hospital nearly every day for weeks. The message said to dial zero for the extension. That was the emergency department.

"What is it?" Caroline asked.

The girl was young. Clearly she hadn't been through anything serious enough yet to have a number like this embedded in her brain. "I don't know yet."

Alice took the paper through the door behind the counter for privacy. She'd press her luck for the second time today and use the phone on Mrs. Weaver's desk to make the call. It's not like she'd come around this time of the day, but if she did, it'd be fine. They could use her phone for emergencies. Even Mrs. Weaver might consider one of her employees in the hospital an emergency.

She placed the call and gave her name to the woman who answered, explaining her brother had left a message for her. The same woman picked up the call two more times after putting her on hold before she was connected to her brother.

"Alice?" It was Bobby's frantic voice on the other end of the line.

"What's going on? Are you okay?"

"Yeah. Where are you?"

"Ravenwood," she said, hoping her brother didn't need a ride home. The car was still trapped in the parking lot.

"Why are you still at work? Doesn't matter. You need to come quick. Mom was in a car accident."

The words ripped Alice's heart from her chest. She jumped up, and the short cord from the receiver lifted the base of the phone off the desk. "What happened? How bad is she hurt?"

"I don't know. She's in surgery. Just get down here, okay?"

Alice sank back in the chair. She couldn't leave, not without risking the trees anger.

"Alice."

She didn't answer him. Dad had to already be at the hospital with him. Maybe Bobby would come get her.

"Alice?"

"Yeah," she said.

"You coming?"

She hung her head. *'Why is this my life?'*

"I can't," she told him.

"What do you...? Let me guess. Car trouble?"

She nodded even though she knew he couldn't see her. "That's right," she sighed.

There was a lot of irritation in his tone when he spoke again. Bobby knew the real reason she stayed at the inn almost as often as she went home. It had been a glaring topic of argument for them, but he gave up trying to convince her how ridiculously she took things. "Fine."

'That's it? He's not going to lecture me? Yell at me to get to the hospital already?'

"I'm going to tell dad I got ahold of you. If your car still won't start," he said with tense anger covering his words, "call me back. I'll come get you."

"Thank you," she whispered. There was a click, and the call disconnected.

Alice stopped at the desk and filled Caroline in on what happened.

"The room wasn't slept in. It'll just be between us. No one will charge you for tonight."

That was kind of her to do. She'd get in a lot of trouble if Mrs. Weaver ever found out.

She almost forgot about her nightgown, but stopped off at the laundry room to grab it after getting her suitcase from the room. She walked back to the employee entrance and stepped outside. The wind whipped her head to the side as soon as she emerged. It hadn't eased up at all.

Alice was about to turn around to call Bobby, but she noticed how clear the sidewalk was when she looked down. Lifting her head, the lot near where she parked didn't have a single leaf, piece of paper, or scattered anything blowing across it. She turned toward the lane and what little she would see of this end of it through the trees was free of debris too.

'That's why my clothes turned up when they did.'

Before she could talk herself out of it, she got in her car and started driving away. The entire lane was empty. Leaves swirled through the air and landed on either side, missing the pavement entirely. When she neared the end of the lane, she checked the rearview mirror and saw everything blowing across behind her. The trees had made her a path.

'Be good to the trees. They will treat you how you treat them.'

The words popped into her head like an old memory, but she couldn't remember where she heard them. It didn't matter if someone had told her that or if she made it up. What mattered was the trees had decided to let her leave.

Chapter Twenty
Baby Charlotte

Meredith pressed her back to the cabin and stood quietly next to the open window. The men were discussing her fate which is why they ordered her outside, out of ear shot. They trusted she wouldn't wander far unsupervised. This far inland there were too many threats for any sane person to run. Between the wild animals and near constant threat of natives, there was safety in numbers.

'It is amusing they think me to be sane.'

Those weren't the biggest threats out here. Even the natives didn't venture far onto this edge of the Weavers' land. When relations were still friendly with them, they had warned of unimaginable dangers in these woods. If one ventured too far, they were never seen again, dead or alive, and would meet a most unfortunate end.

'How would anyone know if they were never seen again?'

The woods were her one hope for escape if this conversation turned the way she feared it would. She was brought here to the hunting cabin far away from the village for them to dispose of her. It would be unlikely, even for louses such as these, to end the life of a woman carrying a child, but being sold to a native tribe wasn't out of the realm of possibility.

"We must act now. The creature growing within her will be

granted freedom anon."

That was the voice of Reverend Standish. He had preached to her every day since her sin was discovered. It haunted her dreams.

"There is still time. Isaac Rolfe shall return ere long."

He was one of the new faces to the group. One of several men she hadn't been acquainted with who were now tasked with deciding her future.

"Thou can't possibly receive her story. She walks with Beelzebub. We might not, but act swiftly."

'The good and righteous Mr. Brewster.' News of Salem had reached their village around the time her belly showed the child she was carrying. He had championed to try her as a witch, to rid their village of evil before it could spread.

"I hast known her since birth. Would we can save her soul, it is the right path." The reverend was one of the few on her side. It wasn't because she mattered, but a win for the good Lord would look favorably upon him if he cast her demons out.

None of them believed her. Things had gone from bad to worse when her fiancé stayed behind in England to tidy up business before she returned to the new land with her family. It was a last minute, much unexpected change of plans.

The night before they were all due to leave England his family sent them off in style. Their plans of dinner weeks before rapidly grew into a party. Meredith's family moved to the new land when she was a child, and she wasn't accustomed to such lavishness. The drink overtook her, and she regretfully, and eagerly, gave in to her fiancé's advances. They were to be married soon after arriving back in the village where her family settled. It was a mistake which would soon be made right with their nuptials.

Everyone in the village was looking forward to the wedding. Life had been much harder than anyone expected, and it gave them hope having such a grand festivity to look forward to, especially between two such prosperous families.

Meredith could feel the presence of the baby in her womb before the boat reached shore. There was time. It would be difficult to explain why the child was born so early, yes, but Isaac was due on one of his merchant boats soon after she arrived.

She busied herself with the planning. When her intended arrived, the wedding preparations needed to be complete if they were to say their vows as soon as possible. Her father raised an eyebrow a time or two, but said nothing. Her mother laughed, "Oh, young love. You miss him so much."

But Isaac never arrived, only his apologies.

It became harder to hide her bulging abdomen. Some secrets were too large to remain hidden. The Weavers never turned her out. They wrote to Rolfe, requesting answers and demanding an audience with him. It took months for him to reply. His letter announced when he would be traveling soon, but ignored the questions of responsibility.

The entire village shunned her and her whole family. She was a disgrace and all of them were shamed by association. They stuck by her, naively believing Isaac would do the right thing.

Brewster and his cohorts insisted on moving her somewhere far reserved from where Rolfe would pass. Her witchery would influence him, sway his tongue to admit crimes he had not committed.

The Weavers brought her here. She'd been in the hunting cabin for a week, waiting on his arrival. Today was when he was expected which brought all manner of men to the property to offer an opinion. They'd been talking for hours. When one of them was almost persuaded she was not a witch, she was cast out of the house until they were finished. They didn't want her influencing their conversation.

'No man will admit the wrong he has done. My fate is sealed.'

In the distance, she could hear a horse's hooves clomp along the dirt path. The messenger was coming to announce Rolfe's arrival in town. Soon after, the men would leave, and Meredith would be left with Mrs. Weaver to wait.

The voices grew louder inside when the messenger came to the door. Chairs were moved, footsteps walked away from the room, and a variety of other clanks and thuds came through the blowing curtains. The excitement filled energy could be felt on the breeze having grown too large for the cabin to contain it. They were all talking at once which made it difficult for Meredith to hear anything.

"What tidings doth thou hast? Hath Rolfe arrived?" It was Mr. Weaver asking.

"Yes," the messenger replied. "He and his newly wed wife."

Meredith couldn't breathe. The words the messenger said were inhaled and lodged in her throat blocking any air from entering her lungs. She tried to take a breath, shoulders lurching forward to aid the air entering through her mouth and nose, but it couldn't get past the invisible obstruction. The wilderness beyond the cabin moved farther away, and she became dizzy, holding on to the outer wall to remain upright. Finally, she gasped hard enough to break through, and her throat burned with physical pain from the force of removing it.

She collapsed to her knees and sank into a sitting position, resting her back against the wall. They hadn't heard her, only because they were too caught up in the argument ensuing from the news the messenger brought. Quiet tears ran in torrents down her cheeks as she listened to these men, some she barely knew, others whose voices she didn't recognize, debate her fate.

For months, she had waited on Isaac. Theirs was not a betrothal set for the benefit of their families, although it would have that affect as well. They loved each other. From the moment their eyes first met, the passion between them was undeniable which easily explained the extra care her father took in chaperoning. That last night in England, however, everyone hit the drink too hard including those watching over her.

'Was he just running away from the ruination of his name?' She prayed to anyone listening he was a coward. Isaac Rolfe wasn't man enough to face his mistakes and pay for them alongside her. *'It can't be he didn't truly love me.'*

Although she had been shunned by the village, she still heard the talk. Whispers between women whom she used to call friends whenever she walked by. Voices lowered just enough to intend they weren't meant to be heard, but still loud enough for her ears. They meant for her to listen to what they had to say.

Isaac had dishonored her because that was all he had wanted in the first place. Meredith Weaver was not the caliber of woman he had desired to marry. She hadn't believed them. Instead she held her head high believing he would be by her side once more.

The voices in the cabin were discussing when to send her back to England. From there, distant relatives would take her to France where there may still be hope of finding a decent husband who was blind, or uncaring, to the dishonor. It had all been decided except for when she should depart.

"Would she leaves now both she and the baby shall die in childbirth during the trip!" her father yelled, interrupting her grief for her engagement.

"It's harsh, yet it might be for the-" Brewster began.

There was a loud crash, and her father sternly warned, "It would be wise for thou not to finish thy thought."

Meredith pulled herself up and stood as close to the window as she dared. They would ship her away from her family after her child was born, but they hadn't yet decided what to do with the babe. When the conversation took a dark turn to how many infants die during birth and how the right midwife could help in that endeavor, she bolted.

There was only one place she could go. There was one place where none of these men, not even her father, was brave enough to follow. She lifted the bottom of her nightgown and ran barefooted into the trees. Inside the cover of the woods, she looked back. There were no faces in the darkness. They were too busy arguing her future to worry about her present. None of them were aware she'd gone. By the time it was discovered, it'd be too late.

Branches smacked at her face and arms. The brush pecked at her nightgown leaving it a tattered shard of the garment she had been wearing. The tears flowed endlessly, and the pain was ignored. Her mind was overrun with agony from the words which kept repeating silently between her ears. "He and his newly wed wife."

This child growing within her was theirs. If only he saw her, if he could see her protruding abdomen which swelled with the life they created, surely, he would not reject her then. *'But he must.'* A pain ripped into her side and she rested against a tree. He was married. He had given his name to another woman.

There was a pull in front of her. Meredith had no concept of how long she had been running or which direction was the way back to the cabin. There was an energy ahead calling to her, pulsating a vibrant light, leading the way. That was where she must go. It was where she and her child would be safe.

It kept moving as she ran toward it causing her to weave and turn. Sometimes it forced her to double back to where she had been. *'Stop moving!'*

Meredith was out of breath and exhausted when she broke through the trees into a small clearing. She dropped to the ground gasping and wheezing. One by one the aches and pains she had amassed made themselves known. The light of the full moon shone brightly down upon her. Her feet were caked in dirt and blood. Streaks of red ran down her arms. She felt the stream of blood running down her inner thigh over her knee before shooting off into several distributaries coursing over her lower leg. She hiked her nightgown higher and higher until she saw the source of her own blood. That's when she felt the pain.

She collapsed on her back with her knees bent and screamed wildly into the open night air. The pulsating vibrant energy found her, encircling her, but she wasn't afraid. Something inside her head cautioned it came for her life, but she welcomed it. Perhaps this was the fate she deserved, to die alone giving birth to a child only cared about by herself.

The screams were heard by the trees who did nothing to comfort her or ease her pain. Hours passed with the moon traveling across the night sky. It was her means for tracking time. She grew weaker and begged for an end to it. Let the child be born or the earth to reclaim her still fertile body into the ground long after she expired. The outcome of her pregnancy was no longer a concern.

Her body felt as if it would split in two. The only sensation she could feel with the pain was the blood pooling beneath her as it soaked her nightgown and dried against her skin. The temperature dropped, but the heat of her fever welcomed the relief.

The words she uttered were foreign even to her. She prayed to her God, but when he didn't answer, she called on anyone who would listen. She begged to be relieved of this pain, this night, and would pay any penance for it to end. When she was ready to give up, to allow the darkness to overtake her, to pass out uncaring if she saw the sun rise in the morning, her body finally accomplished what it was built to do, and she felt her baby enter the world. Meredith sobbed violently, not because it was over, but because she believed it had only just begun.

She rolled to her side and pulled herself into a sitting position. The woods around her swayed, and she almost fell back. The baby lay still and quiet on the ground.

A girl, she smiled. She had longed for a girl to spoil and dress up. The combination of Rolfe and Weaver blood should've made this child a beautiful and sought after bride for any man of good breeding when she came of age.

Meredith scooped her up and wiped off the baby's face. The cord was around her neck, and she quickly unwrapped it allowing her baby to suck in its first breath. She stuck her fingers in her mouth, clearing it of anything which may be blocking her airway. The baby still didn't make a noise.

'Don't panic.' She had watched her mother assist a birth on a ship during one of their trips to England. It took what felt like a worrisome length of time before the child cried, but he did cry. She repeated everything her mother and the midwife did, but nothing worked.

In the moonlight, she could see the bluish hue on her face darkening. She turned the baby over, holding the tiny creature on her stomach in one hand and gently patted her back with the other. Nothing.

A soul crushing wail flew from her lips. It sounded loud enough to be heard at the cabin, in the village, and even aboard the ships in passage between lands. She clutched her baby to her chest and rocked back and forth as the little energy she had continued to fade.

Unable to hold herself upright any longer, she lay back on the ground, nestling the baby next to her. "Charlotte," she whispered to the cherub face whose eyes would never see her mother.

Her eyes blinked open and closed. It was becoming harder to stay awake. The wetness between her legs was growing at an alarming rate. Her bleeding wasn't stopping; it was increasing. The pains lessened only as consciousness became harder to maintain. Meredith fought to stay awake as long as she could, enjoying the sight of the baby, her baby who was the only person in the world who might have loved her still after all she had done.

As the dark of night changed to a lighter shade of blue, she closed her eyes for good. She welcomed death to come, to take her along with her child to whatever afterlife may await them.

Hours later, the song of the birds entered her dreams, and she blinked her eyes open. The sun was bright through the trees, but the branches prevented it from shining directly in her eyes. Several moments passed before she remembered where she was and why. The nightmare of the night before flooded in all at once.

Meredith sat up and looked at the ground where she had laid Charlotte the night before, but the baby was gone. In her place, there stood a sapling which had sprouted during her sleep. She was almost certain it hadn't been there during her labors, but she couldn't be certain of much anymore.

One thing was definite. She was no longer with child. Her belly had flattened to its previous form which seemed unlikely, but every time she ran her fingers over it, there was no evidence she had been with child when she awoke yesterday.

Meredith rose to her feet and scoured the clearing. There was no sign of Charlotte anywhere. "It couldn't have been animals," she said to herself. "I would have woken." She convinced herself the animals would've attacked her body as well.

Her dress was clean and not the nightgown she had been wearing when she fled into the woods. *I'm dead,'* she thought, kneeling on the ground. The sapling reached for the light breaking through the tree tops, and Meredith studied it. "I'm dead," she repeated out loud. "Witches took my baby for use in their hexes and planted a blackthorn tree in her place."

'Or,' she shuddered. If she had unknowingly given birth next to the sapling last night, it would explain the loss of her

child. Meredith shook her head. *'She would still be here if that were true.'*

She was unwilling to accept responsibility for her baby's demise. The fault lied upon the men at the cabin. *'And with Isaac.'*

The clothing she wore was harder to explain. She stood walked the length of the trees at the edge of the clearing while she thought. The trees seemed closer than they had in the dark. They also formed a circle like they had been planted in a specific order for a purpose she didn't recognize. It had to be the pain of childbirth playing tricks on her memory. *'This is what I wore, but where is Charlotte.'*

She went back to the sapling, mesmerized. It called to her in a way she could never explain and would never explain if she had the words and was given the opportunity. As she tried to clear her head, make sense of her memories versus the reality she awoke in, and decide what move to make, the trees spoke to her for the first time. It was then she realized her nightmare had only just begun.

More by Jennifer Lush
The Elementals Series
Air

Lilah is not at all pleased about her family's move to the Midwest regardless of the circumstances behind why they were summoned. It's unfair she has to trade in her days in the sun on the beach for the lackluster cornfields and bare trees filled autumn. Especially since it is centuries old rules and traditions dictating her family's code.

That is until she meets Jackson. The timing of events couldn't be more wrong. Secrets are revealed and psychic powers unleashed as she comes into her own while navigating the diminishing fine line between family honor and independence. Will she be able to help the other Elements fight the unknown force hunting them down while forging her own identity?

Air is the first book in The Elementals series revealing the truth behind myths and legends dating back millennia. Time is running out for the four to bring about the Return and restore Balance to the earth.

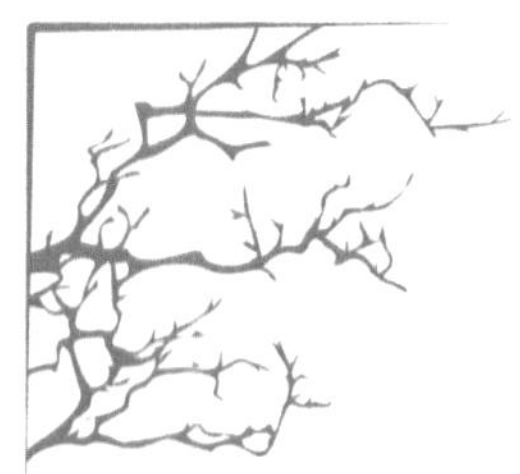

Earth

Everleigh is torn between her grandma's old fashioned ways and wanting to unite the Elementals in the fight to save their people. The vampires are being hunted, and it's only a matter of time before the unknown assailants begin their attack on the witches. Even the best kept secrets have to be revealed if they hope to conquer the storm headed their way.

New witches are being called at an alarming rate which only solidifies what they already know. The fate that awaits them will be cold and deadly. Aligning themselves with a family of immortal psychics gathered near the town could be their only hope to succeed in the fight for survival. Will she be able to help convince the factions to join together in time?

Earth is the second book in The Elementals series revealing the truth behind myths and legends dating back millennia. Time is running out for the four to bring about the Return and restore Balance to the earth.

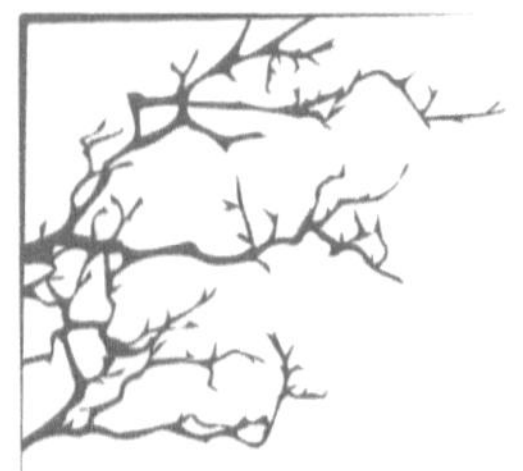

Fire

Judd is torn between two identities. The private life he leads has to remain a secret. It's the only way to save his son. The life he's known by is a past filled with carnage and intimidation. His people are being hunted, and he has to figure out a way to save them without putting his family at risk.

There was a time when vampires roamed all corners of the earth doing as they pleased. Too many times, hunts raged to murder the foul beasts that existed with the humans. The Council created rules that would keep order amongst the clan preventing future onslaught, but now the Council was being targeted as well. Will Judd find who is behind these attacks before the entire clan has fallen?

Fire is the third book in The Elementals series revealing the truth behind myths and legends dating back millennia. Time is running out for the four to bring about the Return and restore Balance to the earth.

Available on Kindle Vella
Ravenwood: Volume Two

Pick up where you left off with more short stories about Ravenwood! Along Route 116 where the state road weaved its way through the backwoods of Massachusetts was the lane leading to Ravenwood. It was easy to miss. The only travelers in that area were either lost or looking for the old Europeanesque inn. The only people who traveled west of Ravenwood were the people who had grown up there. They knew the woods, feared the creatures who dwelled there, but they respected them. They had made friends with the woods for it were the trees who wouldn't let you leave.

The Elementals: Water

The Elements were spiritual entities behind the veil until they materialized corporeally to experience human life. One year was the time frame they were allotted, but it stretched into centuries. Their undoing is at hand, but they must first find out who is trying to bring them down. Water follows the fourth Element's journey from the other side to the beginning of the fight for her kind. Will the Elements finally be able to put their past behind them to fight for their lineage's survival?

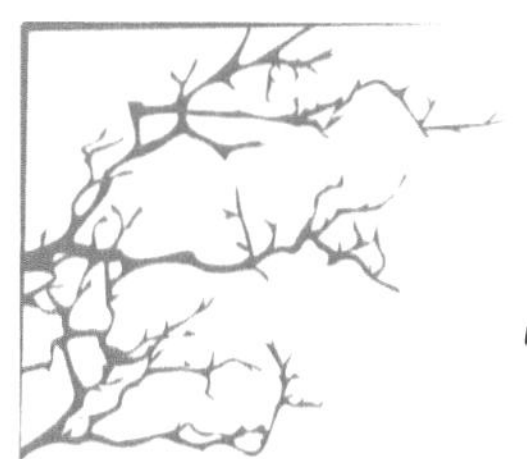

The Below

All manner of supernatural and mythical beasts dwell in The Below. Their refuge underground has kept them safe for centuries. Their world is failing and more of their kind are ascending to the surface. Season one follows Phillipe. He had always known he would never go to The Above. He was the last of his kind, and he hadn't always followed the rules. He accepted this as his fate until he learned the truth about his parents. Their murder and the lies that covered it up sparked an outrage. There was only one way justice would be carried out, and that was by Phillipe's own hands.

Fogpoint Harbor

Kat was surprised to learn of her great-aunt's death twenty years after she had been led to believe Aunt Dot had passed away. As the soul inheritor of the estate, there was a catch. She had to live in her aunt's house for one year to collect. The mysteries surrounding her aunt didn't end with why she had been lied to about her death. Recruited by the police to solve a town's murder, Kat relies on an unlikely source to solve the crime: the ghosts residing in her aunt's Victorian home.

About the Author

Jennifer Lush is a mother of three from central Illinois where she has lived her entire life. Aside from spending time with her children and grandchildren, writing and traveling are her two main consuming passions. Luckily, they are mutually beneficial.

Writing has always been in her blood even if it took her longer than planned to do it. One of her earliest memories of longing to be an author happened in kindergarten when she told her parents what she wanted to be when she grew up. It took close to four decades, but she has finally made that childhood dream come true.

Jennifer is an entertainer at heart who is always making those around her laugh. She can turn any mundane event into a story worth repeating with flair. Inspiration for her fictional worlds comes from everywhere. There are more ideas floating through her mind than she has time to write, but she is determined to finish as many as possible.

Twitter: AuthorJLush
IG: AuthorJenniferLush
Tik Tok: AuthorJenniferLush

Also by Jennifer Lush

Ravenwood
Ravenwood

The Elementals
Air: The Elementals Book One
Earth: The Elementals Book Two